Hard Winter at Broken Arrow Crossing

Hard Winter at Broken Arrow Crossing

Stephen Bly

CROSSWAY BOOKS • WHEATON, ILLINOIS
A DIVISION OF GOOD NEWS PUBLISHERS

Hard Winter at Broken Arrow Crossing

Published by Crossway Books, a division of
Good News Publishers, Wheaton, Illinois 60187.

Cover illustration: Den Schofield

First printing, 1991

Printed in the United States of America

Library of Congress Cataloging-in-Publication Data

Bly, Stephen, 1944-
Hard winter at Broken Arrow Crossing / Stephen Bly.
p. cm.
I. Title.
PS3552.L93H37 1991 813'.54—dc20 91-11345
ISBN 0-89107-620-4

99 98 97 96 95 94 93 92 91
15 14 13 12 11 10 9 8 7 6 5 4 3 2 1

For a list of other books by
Stephen Bly
or information regarding speaking engagements
write:
Stephen Bly
Winchester, Idaho 83555

For
my good friend
WILL CANE
whom
I first met
around noon
summer
of
1952

ONE

Sometime before darkness or death, Stuart Brannon had to find Broken Arrow Crossing.

He considered tying the bandana around his left hand. The numb, bare flesh of three fingers stuck out from the stiff, worn leather glove. But his nose and ears felt worse. The sharp pain stage had ceased hours before, and now a dull, mind-deadening throb signaled real trouble.

Jerking the red bandana up over his face, Brannon futilely attempted to keep the blowing snow from slicing into his skin. His eyes, frost-covered and nearly frozen shut, strained to scout the blizzard for a trail. With black hat tilted low, he saw very little. Brannon's right hand was jammed deep into a coat pocket; his left hand encircled the slim horn of the Visalia saddle. The reins laced through the second and third fingers. That much he could see . . . but couldn't feel.

Sage plodded through the Colorado winter. The white blaze on his black nose pointed straight down. The howl of the storm muffled any other noise. The horse . . . the rider . . . creeping through the lifeless forest. Alone.

Brannon had no guess as to the time of day. Every hour mirrored the one before. A jagged, haunting gray storm welcomed the dawn, and nothinghad improved since then. He didn't bother to stop and eat. It looked impossible to build a fire. His grub bag hung empty anyway.

The color of the sky, the storm, and the ground were all the same. Two feet of fresh snow greeted each step. On some hilltops they stumbled onto ground blown bare by the wind. But the draws and gullies collected drifts up to four or five feet.

Brannon knew the trail would follow the contour of the stream bed. If he held onto his hat with his right hand and squinted straight into the storm, he could barely discern the direction of the river.

At times, during the days he had ridden right up its frozen surface. It cracked and twanged in the strange way that only a frozen body of water can. But even the fresh snow couldn't keep Brannon and Sage from slipping on the lightning-quick glass surface. They slid their way back off the river and onto what trail there was left to follow.

The station at Broken Arrow Crossing would be closed for the winter. But Brannon had been told that Everett Davis wintered out at the Crossing, and Davis was supposed to know the location of Charley Imhoff. So Stuart Brannon pushed on. Somewhere up that bleak trail a fire blazed. A soup pot boiled. And surely there was a barn full of hay.

He hadn't spent much of his thirty years thinking about dying.

He was just too busy.

Not that Brannon hadn't looked down the sights of his rifle and revolver a number of times. But survival always concerned him too much to worry about failure.

Twice he had bullets pumped into him.

Once he was knifed in the back.

But those incidents just made him mad.

Now the cold had him bound, body and mind. He began to consider whether death would be less painful than living. If he could spot a big sprawling fir tree, he thought about crawling under the limbs for a long sleep. He knew it would be a long, long sleep. Brannon was worried. The constant freezing temperature was starting to affect his mind as well as his body. It wouldn't let up. There was no break.

He forced himself to think about the future. Spring would be different. These mountains would be beautiful. Big outfits would be searching the streets for hands. Any man who could throw a rope would be hired on the spot. One as experienced as Brannon . . . would be made foreman.

But spring was a faraway dream.

So was Arizona Territory.

He held back the reins on Sage and slowly climbed down into dry, powdery snow that was too cold to stick to his clothes. He shuffled up in front of the black gelding and began to lead him through the blizzard. There is a point of communication between horse and rider that goes deeper than sight, sound, or touch. He knew, by habit, that it was time to give Sage a rest.

After intense rubbing, Brannon straightened out his left hand. When the fingers began to bend on their own, he loosened the cinch.

Banging the snow off his hat on his knee, he pulled off the remnant of his left glove and ran his fingers through his brown hair. *Man, it feels frozen, grimy, and long.*

He tried to speak to the horse, but no sound came out of his throat. Instead, he patted sage's neck, passed the reins to his right hand, and jabbed his frozen left hand into his pocket.

Pausing on the top of the second incline, Brannon leaned against the animal's withers, letting Sage block some of the severity of the wind. Suddenly the horse reared his head and nervously searched the landscape. Brannon stepped in front to calm him.

Smoke!

He couldn't see it, but he could smell it. Brannon immediately turned in what he presumed was the direction of the river. Dragging Sage at the slow end of the reins, Brannon stumbled into a little grove of aspens, grotesque white fingers groping through the air. Then they brushed by some pines into a clearing. Somewhere in the blinding sameness of the horizon, he thought he saw the outline of a building.

With a final surge of energy, he and Sage plowed through the snow until they reached the large, rough door of a barn. He pulled the horse in and shoved the door shut. For a moment, he just stood still, breathing deep, enjoying the abrupt relief from the blowing snow.

Brannon located a lantern hanging near an empty stall, but he had no matches. He felt his way along, gradually becoming adjusted to the darkness. It was a long barn with at least a half dozen stalls on each side of a wide center room. In the middle was an old wagon propped up on barrels, wheels missing. In fact, all the stalls seemed empty.

All except one.

He almost tripped over the dropped horse. He knelt close to hear labored breathing and rattling lungs. He choked out a raspy whisper. "They rode him in the ground." He felt his way back to Sage who stood still beside the door. He led the horse to a stall and pulled off the saddle and bridle. Finding an empty grain sack, he and rubbed down the laboring black horse. After a few minutes, he climbed the ladder to the loft and tossed down an arm load of hay.

Brannon was tempted to crawl back into the loft and collapse. But he felt driven to find the owner of the dying horse.

He shoved the door open and threw himself back out into the squalling wind. Circling the building, he discovered that the living quarters consisted merely of a cabin attached to one end of the barn.

He banged on the door and then shoved it open with his shoulder. His eyes caught a glow in the fireplace. Even in the semidarkness, he could see the floor strewn with pots, pans, clothes, and food. He started toward the fire but stopped short when he noticed an old man stretched out on a bunk.

The man's eyes were closed. "I'm looking for Everett Davis. Do you mind if I borrow a little warmth of that fire?"

Stuart Brannon never made it to the fire. At once, he heard the sound of splintering wood as a blow slammed into the back of his head.

Then he heard nothing at all.

The rough wood floor of the cabin felt icy-hard, and dirty. Brannon rubbed his throbbing head and struggled to push himself to his hands and knees. He had no idea how long he had been unconscious. The oppressive grayness of the storm had vanished into a coal-black night. The fire was out.

Pulling what was left of his gloves from his hands, he rubbed his eyes and his week-old beard. He sat back on his knees, refusing to get to his feet until his vision improved. Desperately he tried to recall the layout of the cabin.

There's a wall . . . a shelf . . . a lantern.

"Hey. You on the floor . . . you comin' to?"

Brannon yanked his gun from the holster and ducked down without saying a word.

The labored voice broke the silence again.

"Look . . . if you're plannin' on shooting me, you're too late. I've been back-shot. I came to before the fire died and saw you lying there, but I can't get off the bed. Did he shoot you too?"

Brannon cleared his throat, "No, but he used my head to make kindling out of your chair. Are you Everett Davis?"

"Why . . . do you want to know?" The man on the bed coughed, then groaned.

"I'm Stuart Brannon, a friend of Charley Imhoff's."

"You don't say . . . are you the old boy that fought the Apaches at Mission Springs?"

"Yeah, Charley and I were there. Did he tell you about that?"

"Shoot, everyone north of the Colorado has heard the story. Charley's made you out to be a legend."

"That sounds like him."

"He said you hand-fought two of them with a six-inch blade stuck in your back. Is that right?"

"That's what they tell me. I've never been much of one to count coup like Charley. Where's the lantern? At least we can get some light going. I suppose our friend's gone. He must have been in a hurry to get somewhere to shove out at night into a storm like this."

"He was in a hurry, all right. Look over on that distant wall, two-thirds the way up . . . ought to be an oil lamp hanging there, providin' he didn't take it. And watch your head; the beams sag over on that side."

"No doubt he took my horse. His was near dead."

Brannon groped toward the wall, jerked back to regain his footing, and cracked his head.

"That beam's right at six feet," the old man on the bed announced. "You must be a tall one."

Brannon fumbled with the lantern and then searched for the matches. His hands were no longer numb, but they ached with the sudden rush of blood.

He hung the lit lantern on a hook in the middle of the room and picked up the knocked-over table and benches.

Flickering shadows lay on the man in the bed, but Brannon could see wild gray hair. Dark eyes stared at him from under a buffalo robe.

"Let me see that wound," he said, his deep voice sounding near normal.

"Well, sir, you're going to have to roll me over. I can't move my legs, and my hands are going numb. You see, I was reaching up for my rifle when he back-shot me."

The old man let out a scream as Brannon rolled him to his

side. He pull up the blood-soaked rawhide shirt and stood back to get the full advantage of the light.

"The hole looks clean enough, and the bleeding is slowing. But you've lost a lot of blood, and it looks like it ripped you deep. Probably lodged up against your backbone."

"You've cut bullets out, ain't ya?" the old man asked.

"Yeah, I've cut out bullets, arrowheads, and porcupine quills, but there is no way I could go that deep. Only a doctor would know where to dig for that one."

"You got to do it, Brannon. If I lose circulation, gangrene will set in. I've seen it happen."

"Yeah, and I've seen well-intentioned cowboys kill their best friends trying to play doctor. Don't ask me to carve your funeral. If we can get your circulation going, maybe it will work out a bit. Think about it. Would you want to cut that deep into a guy?"

"Only that bushwhacker."

Brannon found a fairly clean flour sack on the far side of the cabin. He soaked it in a pail of water by the rough rock fireplace and wrung the water out on the floor. Then he pressed it tight against the wound and pulled up the robe.

"Well, ain't you goin' to turn me over and prop me up?"

"I think you better get some rest just like that."

Everett Davis pushed up on his elbows and groaned. "And I say a guy's got a right to die sittin' up and lookin' at his own cabin."

Brannon obliged the older man. Then he rebuilt the fire.

"You got anything to eat? I'm not much of a cook, but right now I could eat my boots."

"Well, if it's still standing, there should be some beans soaking in the pot and some sourdough bread in a skillet that fell off the table."

"Who was that guy? What did he want?"

"Don't know his name. Do know he was looking for gold."

"Gold? You keep gold around here?"

"Brannon, if I had gold in this place, I'd take off and spend the winter in Denver or San Francisco."

"So why did he think there was gold?"

"It's your old friend Imhoff. Charley came into Tres Casas about the first of October talking of finding gold up on the Little Yellowjacket. Well, his timing was bad 'cause the Rutherford brothers and that bunch had been on a two-week drunk. Anyway, the next morning Charley was dead, and he didn't have any gold left on him."

"Charley's dead?" Brannon jerked around and stared at the man on the bunk.

"Six shots in him, I hear."

"What about the gold strike?"

"Well, folks around Tres Casas started to swarm the Little Yellowjacket. But an early storm hit, and it hasn't let up since. Some of them knew I was a friend of Charley's. So even though the stage station was snowed in for the winter, a few of them have made it up here to pry out of me where the gold came from."

"And this guy pried too hard?"

"He came in wild. Acted like a wounded bear that's lost it's reason. Rippin', tearin', shootin', cussin', all before I knew what was going on. Gold fever, I guess."

"Did you tell him where to find the gold?"

"That's assumin' I know. I haven't seen Charley in over a year."

After the two ate, Everett Davis closed his eyes and drifted in and out of sleep. Brannon carried the lantern out to the barn. Within moments he returned.

"Everett, you awake? The storm hasn't let up a bit," he said as he balanced an arm load of logs for the fire. "It's just as I figured. My horse is gone, and his is dead. Sage won't last long in this weather."

Trying to improve his circulation, Davis slapped the

palms of his hands together several times. Then he laid his left arm across his forehead and again shut his eyes. "Only a crazy man would ride out at night in a storm like this."

"Well, back-shooting doesn't seem to be a mark of clear thinking," Brannon added. "Where are you keeping the station horses? That barn's empty."

"The company only keeps three horses up here through the winter. A dozen Utes showed up about a week back. They wanted to trade for the horses, but I just chased them off. Next morning, the horses disappeared. I felt stranded, thinkin' I wouldn't see another soul until the spring thaw."

"You should have been so lucky. Got any snowshoes?"

"Sure, up above your head."

"They'll probably get me through better than Sage. It's a fierce storm. What direction is the Little Yellowjacket?"

"Straight east, but I don't think anyone could get through the pass."

"That means he'll have to turn around and come back here?"

"Providing he's not froze, lost, or headed back down to Tres Casas. But it's not likely he could make it back to town."

"Well, I'm not going to sit here waiting for him to start shooting. I'm going after him at daybreak. No man on earth steals my horse and rides away."

Brannon threw a couple of big logs on the fire. Then he shook the dust off a blanket and tossed it across another bunk that was about as wide as a deacon's bench, built into the cabin wall near the door.

He slept in spurts. Pain, anger, sorrow, and hopelessness took their turns wrestling in his dreams.

By the time daylight changed the darkness into a depressing lighter hue, Stuart Brannon had bundled himself up and laced on the snowshoes. Though still exhausted from weeks of hard traveling, he found renewed determination.

It was always that way. He could always find a purpose, a reason for pushing through one more day, one more week.

Four times he drove the big herds from south Texas to Kansas. Each drive brought him twenty head of his own. With eighty-five head of Texas longhorns, he accomplished the impossible. Stuart Brannon drove them up the Rio Grande to Las Cruces and then across the Territory to the Mogollon Plateau. By the time he reached Red Rock Canyon, most all the settlers and half the Apaches knew his name. The Indians called him, "The-One-Who-Does-Not-Turn-Back."

The land agent warned him that the country was too wild to be settled. Brannon proved him wrong.

The people in town told him Lisa Nash was too spoiled by an eastern college to want to be a ranch wife. He proved them wrong too.

For the past few weeks, Brannon's world had been behind him. Now, if only to catch a horse thief, his life was up ahead, and that, more than hours of rest, gave him the strength to push on out into the storm once more.

"Everett, you've got food on the bench by your bed, and your Sharps is loaded and lying alongside of you. Don't try to get up. If that back-shooter comes through the door, level him with your rifle, and then try to find out what happened to me. I might not be gone too long. If the trail looks hopeless, I'll be back by noon."

"Stuart Brannon, you watch him. He won't go by the rules."

"Listen, keep those arms and hands moving today. Don't let them stove-up on you. Practice wiggling your toes."

"Yeah, talk about an exciting day . . . I ought to go out there with you."

"Sure, you might make good wolf bait. How much they paying for pelts this year?"

Brannon shouldered the door and waved at Davis. The

storm had slowed just enough to get a good view of the trees along the river. He had intended to head due east into the rising sun. But with such a heavy storm still hanging in the mountains, east was hard to find.

When he left the cabin, he had no doubts about finding the trail or getting his horse and saddle by night. It wasn't until the fierce cold of the day seeped back into his hands and feet that he began to consider the real difficulty ahead.

He had hiked three hours through the blustering storm and finally started thinking about turning back. The wind, while much weaker than the day before, displayed the strength to cover up tracks. He didn't want to lose his way back to the cabin.

I'll just crest that hill. If there's no sign, I'll quit.

But there was no trace of horse or rider. So then he decided just one more hill, and then just one more. Stuart Brannon knew that if he didn't turn around soon, he wouldn't be able to make it back to the cabin before dark.

He also knew he would never turn back until he regained his horse or caught the man who stole him.

Finally, the storm recessed, and he discovered a small aspen with most of the bark freshly chewed off at the three-foot level.

That horse is starving.

He stalked a circle out from the tree looking for another sign. About a hundred feet to the left, another tree had been nibbled. Sighting in a line from the two, he headed up the hill.

At the top of the mountain, he thought he spotted a glimmer of flame from downhill. Brannon stood still and watched as the storm picked back up. Finally, he isolated a column of smoke. He inched forward as his right hand rested on the ice-cold handle of his holstered Colt.

As he neared a grove of snow-heavy pines, he stopped and unlaced the snowshoes. He left them propped against a tree and plowed his way on through the snow. Somewhere ahead of him waited smoke, fire, and trouble.

Stuart Brannon always assumed the worst. That's why he moved in slowly, tree by tree, figuring it could just as well be a band of Ute Indians as a lone gunman. A few minutes later, he caught sight of a thin spiral of smoke, then an outline of a horse lying in the snow. He slipped the .45 out of his holster.

He was counting on Sage not picking up his scent.

He was counting on Sage being alive.

Beside the downed horse, a figure huddled over a small fire built in the stump of a rotted tree. Brannon eased forward. He never took his eye or his aim off the squatting man who had a saddle blanket wrapped over his head and shoulders, trying to trap all the warmth of the fire.

Suddenly, all three moved at the same time. Sage raised his head and whinnied. The man under the blanket spun around, grabbing for his holstered gun. Stuart Brannon cocked the hammer of his Colt with his thumb and shouted above the storm, "Don't try it!"

The man froze in place, half kneeling, hand still beside his firearm.

"Who are you?" he growled.

Brannon studied him, straight and steady. "You stole my horse and saddle, left me unconscious next to an old man you back-shot. That's who I am!"

"But you aren't going to just walk in here and shoot me, are ya?"

"For stealing my horse, I could shoot you in the head, or I could shoot you in the gut, or I could shoot you in the heart."

"I had to borrow your horse. You can have it back."

"Mighty generous now that you've near pushed him to death."

"Look, just back off. Let's talk about this. It could be

worth a lot to you. Gold. I've got a claim up on the Little Yellowjacket."

"Yeah, I hear you're trying to claim-jump a good friend of mine, Charley Imhoff."

"Imhoff's dead. . . ."

Brannon shoved his gun within inches of the man's head.

"I didn't kill him! His claim's up for grabs, and I know where it is. You, being a friend, can halve it with me. All we got to do is establish ourselves up there during the winter. Then, when all those shop clerks come overrunning the area, we'll have our claim secure."

Brannon didn't flinch. He didn't lower the gun. He didn't blink. He laid the cold barrel against the man's temple. "Where'd you get directions to the claim?"

The man under the saddle blanket eased down to his knees away from the pointed gun. "The old man back at the cabin gave 'em to me right before he died."

Stuart Brannon stood pat. "So you admit you shot Everett Davis?"

"Hey, the old man had it coming. He had shoved that Sharps at me, threatened to blow my head off, so I went for my gun in self-defense. Honest."

Brannon noticed that the man's eyes darted to search the trees behind him. *He's looking to make his move.*

Stuart Brannon's shouted words echoed across the storm. "Everett Davis got shot in the back. I just tended his wound, and he's not dead yet. Now, you're wanting to grab that gun of yours, and I'm telling you not to do it. So move real slow, and raise your hands away from that holster. Maybe you've shot men in the back, but it's a whole lot different when you're looking down the barrel of a cocked .45."

The man's hands started up. Then he yanked the saddle blanket from his shoulders and threw it at Brannon, going for his holster all in one motion. But two bullets blazed from

Brannon's gun before the saddle blanket ever hit him. The man rocked back across the fire and didn't move.

Seconds. The whole scene lasted just seconds, and now a man lay dead. Brannon turned him over in the snow.

This was the part of life in the West that Stuart Brannon liked least.

Too few options when law, decency, and morality are left up to us. This old boy figured to shoot his way to riches.

"Well, mister, I sure wish you hadn't done that. I can't even give you a burial in this storm. And I sure can't put you on Sage. But I'll be back."

He retrieved his snowshoes and then coaxed Sage to his feet. The horse lost his footing and almost went back down. Brannon slapped him on the rump and bullied him forward. He grabbed the saddle and blanket and sludged back through the snow, towing Sage behind.

Twice he lost the trail.

Twice Sage slumped into the deep drifts.

The snow continued to fall, but the wind died down. It was near dark when he sighted the barn and cabin.

After taking care of his horse, Brannon went back to the cabin to check on Everett Davis.

"You going to tell me about it?" Davis asked.

"About what?"

"About how you got your horse back."

"I took it away from him."

"I don't suppose he liked that much?"

"Nope."

"Was there shootin'?"

"Yep."

"His gun, or yours?"

"Just mine."

"Is he dead?"

"Yeah. . . ."

"Brannon, gettin' words out of you is like pullin' teeth. How's your horse?"

"Barely alive."

"But the horse will pull through, right?"

"Maybe, but it'll be two weeks before he should be ridden. Can you hang on that long? How are you feeling?"

"Well, my hands are normal, and my feet seem to be warmer. As long as I don't move much, I can make the month out. But there's no way I can travel down the mountain to Tres Casas."

"If the snow lets up and that horse survives, I'll go down and bring you up a doc."

"This storm will close Brighten Pass." Davis added, "I don't think anyone can get through to Tres Casas 'til late March."

"I can make it."

"Well," Davis hesitated, "that might be, but there ain't a doc tough enough to climb back up here."

Brannon ladled some beans into a skillet, fried some venison with them, and opened a can of peaches he found rolled back under his bunk. He ate sitting on the bench in the middle of the room.

Davis scraped his plate clean with a knife and cleared his throat. "What I want to know is, what is some rancher from Arizona doing up here in Colorado in the middle of a blizzard? Now I know it ain't my business, but Charley Imhoff told me you had a big spread, a fine home, and the most handsome woman west of St. Louis. Yet you come ridin' in here lookin' like some down-and-out drifter."

"Well, you're right about one thing."

"How's that?"

"It's none of your business."

The room was silent for a good five minutes. Then it was Davis who spoke.

"Look, no offense. I just felt like I knew you after all Charley had said."

"Well, I'm here because Charley sent me a letter saying to try to come up as soon as I could. Some deal about making a lot of money."

"He must have meant to cut you in on the claim. But why did you head up here in the dead of winter?"

"Because I had nowhere else to go."

TWO

"Everett, how heavy's a dead horse?"

Stuart Brannon lay on the narrow bunk, plotting his day's work before daylight.

The old man in the bed raised up on one elbow. "About the same as a live one, I reckon. What . . . a thousand, maybe eleven hundred pounds?"

"Where are the wheels for the wagon out in the barn?"

"Tres Casas. Boswick took them in to be re-spoked. They won't be back until spring. But it doesn't sound like your horse could pull it in his condition anyway. It would take a team of draft horses to drag a wagon through this storm."

Brannon stirred around, pulling on his boots. "You got any old barn boards around here?"

"I suppose there's a few, up in the loft. But they're as crooked as a Faro dealer at the Palace."

"How warped are they?"

"Well, if you step on one end, the other will try to punch you in the nose. Why?"

"I've got to get that old boy buried. And then, there's the dead horse to move out of the barn."

"Ain't no way one man can do it . . . especially one without a horse."

"There are some things in life a man's got to do," Brannon shrugged.

The two men talked little during breakfast.

Brannon broke the silence, "I think that block and tackle will stretch back and reach the horse. I could, at least, swing him outside. If I can make a sled, then I'll see if I can drag him downhill."

"That storm sounds bad out there," Davis cautioned.

"Well, I'd better go find that bushwhacker first. I'll pull him back on the same sled. You got any soft ground around here for a burial?"

"Brannon, there's not a foot of soft ground within ten miles of us in the summertime! If this place weren't halfway between Tres Casas and the goldfields, nobody on earth would live here. And this time of the year, even the sand along the river is froze solid!"

"You got a pick and shovel?"

"Check the far wall of the barn. You're going to dig him a grave, aren't you?"

"Yep," Brannon nodded.

"He wouldn't have done it for you or me."

"Nope, I suppose not. Any of your relatives ever gone bad, Everett?"

"A brother of mine spent some time down at A.T.P. in Yuma for robbing a Wells Fargo office," Davis replied.

"Well, what if he would have got shot while attempting the holdup? Would you have wanted someone to bury him?" Brannon pointed his fork at the old man as he talked.

"Yeah, you've got a point."

"That old boy, mean and dumb as he was, has got a brother somewhere who would sure like us to take care of him."

It took Brannon a couple of hours to fashion a makeshift sled out of the barn boards. Using rope for lead lines, he put the snowshoes on and pushed back out into the mountains to find the dead man.

The storm had dumped another six inches of fresh snow, but the wind had died down, and visibility was the best it had been for several days. Brannon found the chewed bark sign on the trees and was surprised to spot smoke still drifting out of the smouldering stump.

The man's snow-covered body sprawled just as Brannon had left it. "Well, at least the wolves didn't eat you." He rolled it over on the sled, lashed it down, and then headed back.

By the time he made it to the cabin, his clothes were soaked clear through with sweat. It was almost dark.

"You look like a train hit you," Everett Davis laughed.

"That's just the man; I haven't got to the horse yet. How did that fire get stirred up?"

"Well, there are just some things a man's gotta do," Everett grinned. "The pain's better today, so I sort of crawled over to the fire."

It took until noon the next day for Stuart Brannon to chip through the frozen rocky soil and dig the grave.

He stomped his snow-covered boots on the porch and reentered the cabin.

"Everett, you got a Bible around here?"

"Now that's one thing I do have. I keep it under my bunk."

Brannon went over and picked up the book and leafed through it. "To tell you the truth . . . well, I just figure a man ought to have the Bible read over him. You got any suggestions what I should read?"

"If he'd have been a good man . . . well, why don't you read Psalm 121. It has something to do with looking up at the mountains. This old boy had his eyes set on the mountains, that's for sure."

The horse took less effort to remove than Brannon had

figured. The hay rope and pulley swung the horse out the front door of the barn and onto the sled. Once he dragged it away from the front of the cabin, it began to slide easily downhill. After getting it moving on its own, Brannon pointed it off the trail towards the rocks far below. Horse and sled made a rapid descent.

The next two days he cut firewood and nursed Sage, who had taken a turn for the worse and had stopped eating. For Stuart Brannon, it was the season of the year to keep busy . . . very busy. Finally, Everett Davis brought up the subject.

"I suppose you know it's Christmas Eve." He sat on the edge of the bed pushing beans across his tin plate.

Brannon stared into the fire. "Yeah, I know."

Both men sat silent for a time.

"Well, I hope you didn't sneak off to town and buy me a new pair of boots or something," Davis chuckled.

"Me?" Brannon joined in. "You're the one to do a thing like that. I bet you sent off to Denver to get me a new saddle."

"You guessed it! One of those hand-tooled jobs with big silver conchos and your name on the cantle."

"With tapaderas?" Brannon teased.

Davis roared, "You want tapaderas? You got it. And a big silver and gold bit for the horse's mouth. With matching spurs for you. You know, with those big old Californio rowels?"

"And," Brannon added, "the sweetest sounding jinglebobs you ever heard."

"Yeah, that's it. That's it, that's what I bought ya. But," Davis added, "seein' that the pass is snowed in, I guess they just won't arrive in time for the holidays."

"Well, Everett, I just sent down to Tres Casas and ordered up a great big smoked ham—"

"With cherry glaze on top?"

"Yeah, that's the one. It must weigh fifty pounds. We'll be

having fried ham for a month. And then I had them send up a hundred-pound sack of Rio Grande sweet potatoes."

"Those big orange ones?"

"Yep. Fresh butter dances across those steaming spuds, and a man can't resist temptation. I even had them ship a bushel of fresh spring peas and a crate of eatin' corn all the way from Mexico. Goes without saying that there will be plenty of fresh milk, eggs, and sugar on that load."

Davis slapped his knee. "Naturally . . . naturally!"

"But here's the surprise. You know the lady that runs the boarding house?"

Everett Davis edged his shoulder toward the fire. "You mean Nadine Montgomery?"

"Is she the one that bakes those good pies?"

"Yeah, she's the one."

"Well, I had the widow Montgomery whip us up twelve!"

"Twelve pies? For just the two of us?"

"Who knows, maybe company will drop in for the holidays? Anyway, there are four deep-dish apple pies, three fresh peach cobblers, two creamy custard pies, two large pumpkin pies with fresh cream to pour over the top, and two huckleberry pies with berries the size of your thumb!"

"Uuuhweee! What a present! But you said she sent twelve pies. I counted thirteen different ones."

"Well, uh, listen . . . everyone knows how the widow Montgomery is sort of sweet on you. She must have slipped another one in just for love."

"Sweet on me? Have you ever seen that lady?"

Brannon tried to stop laughing, "No, I reckon I haven't."

"That woman could whip me and my horse while still stirring a cake. That's one sturdy woman. She looks like she was dropped in tall grass, if you catch my drift."

"Well, now, that's not what I hear." Brannon folded his arms. "But due to the heavy snows, delivery won't be made until April. You don't mind waiting, do you?" Brannon got up and added another log to the fire. "I suppose there's worse places to be on Christmas Eve," he shrugged.

"Well, I spent one winter in Bodie, the first year that field opened up," Davis drawled. "Nothing was up there but a few dugouts and a couple dozen gold-crazy fools. We figured to have all the gold dug out of there in a few weeks. I had planned to get out before the bad weather, but . . . you know, you stick around just one more day expecting to get a little richer. Well, those winds came whipping off the Sierras, and a fella would likely blow all the way to Genoa before he hit ground. No firewood to speak of. I remember wondering if I would ever see another Christmas. I can tell you one thing. When the gold plays out in Bodie, that town's done. It's a horrible place to spend the winter. How about you, Brannon?"

Stuart Brannon stepped slowly to the bench. He leaned back until he stretched flat, hands propped under his head.

"I said, Brannon, it's your turn. Tell me about a good Christmas then," Everett urged.

"No, I'll tell you about the worst of all Christmases. Tonight seems fitting. Just one year ago tonight. I had a nice spread down in Arizona—northwest of St. Johns along Surprise Creek. I came into that country about eight years ago. Drove a little herd up from the Rio Grande.

"Anyway, last Christmas, things were looking pretty good. Had a big stone house on a hill, about eight hundred head of longhorns, and the most beautiful girl in the Territory for my wife. Lisa . . . Lisa Nash."

"She related to the Nashes that own the Green River Land and Cattle Company?" Davis interrupted.

"Yeah, that's an uncle. Well, we had only been married about a year, and she was expecting a baby. Lisa was one of those gals who has everything planned exactly. The baby was due around the middle of February. She didn't want it to interfere with the holidays, she said. She even had it all arranged to travel to Flagstaff and spend the last month with her mother. That way she'd have help, and there were some doctors around, just in case.

"Well . . . come late December, and the storms rolled into our area. It must have rained a foot in less than a day. Arizona country can't handle that much water all at once. There were flash floods everywhere. The bridges to town went out. The roads disappeared. Even some buildings along the creek got washed downstream. It isolated us. But I wasn't too worried, what with the baby not due for a few weeks.

"Of course, I had my hands full with the cattle. They were lost, scattered, bogged down, and wandering about. I'd ride out at daybreak and only come back to the ranch to change horses about noon. Everything being so hectic, still I had it in my mind to come in early on Christmas Eve. I'd spent the afternoon trying to pull an old mossyhorn out of some red clay. When I got home, I was covered with mud from head to toe, and it was way past dark. There wasn't a light on in the place, so I figured the missus was planning a surprise.

"But I heard Lisa screaming for me from the bedroom. I ran in there and found her on the floor. She had started having the baby and collapsed, not able to make it to the bed. Well, I was beside myself. I picked her up and put her right on top the satin comforter.

"I wanted to take her to town, but there was no way to get through, and she sure wasn't up to traveling in a wagon. I thought about riding in and getting the doc, but she didn't want me to leave her. She must have known something.

"Well, I'll tell you, Everett, I'd rather get strung up by the Apaches than go through that. Me, a big strong man setting all muddy on those snow-white sheets, crying my head off 'cause there was nothing I could do to help."

"It was about midnight when the baby came. Lisa had

been in horrible pain until then. I cleaned up a little and got things ready for the baby the best I could.

"I sat there holding her sweet little hand as she had that baby. I mean, I've had my share of pulling calves, horses, and hogs . . . but I've never seen a birth so difficult. When the little fella finally came out . . . "

It was quiet in the cabin for a long time.

Then Brannon started in again. "When he came out, he was dead. Davis, how do you tell your suffering wife that the baby is dead?"

Everett Davis wiped his eyes on his sleeve and remained silent.

"Lisa, uh, well . . . she sort of . . . I guess, just sort of gave up after she heard about the baby. She stared at the ceiling and didn't speak. I sat there holding her in my arms until daybreak, but she had been dead a couple hours by then.

"A year ago tomorrow I was digging two graves. That's why I don't have much use for Christmas . . . just too painful, I guess." Brannon took a small glowing stick out of the fire and lit the lantern. Then he silently put on his coat, grabbed the lantern, and walked out into the night.

He stepped with caution on the packed snow now frozen into solid ice. Swinging the barn door closed behind him, he hung the lantern on a hook and flopped down on the wagon bed. It never crossed his mind to check on his horse. He just lay there staring at the flickering light of the lantern. *One whole year. Sometimes, Lisa, I think you were the lucky one.*

Two hours later Brannon stole back into the cabin.

"It blowed clear out there. You can see a million stars. Everett, you still awake?" he probed.

"Ohm, yeah, I'm just laying here dreaming of one of Mrs. Montgomery's big apple pies."

"Are you sure you aren't missing the widow Montgomery?"

Everett Davis scowled. "Well, a fella gets stuck in the cabin long enough, he can't even control his wishin'."

"What caused you to sit the winter out at Broken Arrow Crossing?" Brannon asked.

Davis shoved his legs over the edge of the bed and sat up the best he could. "Well, I've hung out around this place for three winters now. Wishy Boswick runs a stage and some freight wagons from the end of April to November. Then the passes close over, and he just shuts it down. But he likes to have someone at the station, just looking after the place.

"Wishy and me go way back to that strike in '71 up on Cedar Creek. We partnered up and struck a nice claim that first summer. Sold out for five thousand dollars. They tell me she produced twenty times that amount, but it seemed like a lot to us at the time.

"Well, Wishy was no fool. He headed down to Tres Casas and bought a freight wagon and a load of merchandise and returned right back up to the field. He has been pulling freight, and money, ever since."

Brannon plopped down on his bunk. "What about your half? With that much money you could have bought a couple hundred head of Texas longhorns."

"Now, that's a cattleman talking. You're looking at an old prospector. I was in California in '49 and in Virginia City in '59. After that strike on Cedar Creek, I headed to Denver and tied on a three-day celebration. Then I met up with Princeton Williams. Everyone called him 'the Prince.' Well, he had this idea that there was gold up on Cripple Creek. Somehow, greed got the best of me, and I ended up outfitting the expedition. It was me and 'Prince' and an old Indian named Forever."

"Forever?"

"Yeah, don't that beat all? Well, I found out why folks called him 'the Prince.' He ordered me and that Indian to wait on him hand and foot. Not only that, the two of them got lost and couldn't ever show me where the supposed rich diggings were. By the time I got out of that deal, I was broke again.

"Then I got a job driving freight for Wishy, but it was too confining. I like to get out and do some summer prospecting. So I just winter up here and hit the streams when the ice breaks up. At least, that was my routine before I got myself back-shot."

"But that's only *my* story," Davis continued. "It don't tell us a thing about why *you're* up here. Oh, I know you came because Charley asked you to. Still, that don't tell all the story. Course if you still ain't interested in talking, pay me no mind. I'm just an old man killing time on Christmas Eve."

Brannon swung to the edge of his bunk and peered across the shadows of the cabin. The firelight flickered on the old man's face. He could see beads of sweat forming on his cheeks. Brannon took his bandana and wiped the back of his own neck. He looked down at his hands.

"Everett, you know what I'd like to have for Christmas? A hot bath. Really! Something that would soak the dirt right out of me. Any chance you have a tub around here?"

"I think there's a tin tub out there in the barn. Check all of them stalls. Ain't sure it's ever been used, especially in the winter. I suppose you could pull it right in here and boil some water. But to be honest, you don't look all that dirty."

Even though it was well past dark, Brannon scurried around putting a couple pots of water over the blazing fire. Within a few minutes, he was dragging an oblong tin tub into the center of the room.

Davis inspected it. "It's full of snow!"

"Sure, that's the cold water. Now all we have to do is warm it up." Brannon dumped the hot water into the tub. Within a half-hour the water in the tub was sufficiently warm. Finally, he stripped off his clothes and slowly eased himself in. He hunkered down into the tub with only his powerful shoulders and head sticking out of the water.

"Everett, have you got a straight razor around here?"

"It ought to be over in that box on the shelf. You ain't fixing to shave in the dead of winter, are you?"

"Well, the thought did occur to me. If I keep letting these chin whiskers grow, someone will think we're related."

Everett Davis leaned back on the buffalo robe and sighed, "A man needs some relatives. Most of my kin are in California. Every time I see them, they want to borrow some money. Look at me. Am I the kind of guy who has money to lend? You got any relatives, Brannon?"

"Brother in St. Louis and a sister who married a Frenchman and lives in Mexico City. That's about it. Then I told you about Lisa. Did I tell you about how I ended up in Arizona?"

"No, I . . . er . . . don't believe you did."

"I grew up in south Texas," Brannon began. "Signed on with an outfit when I was just a kid. Drove some of those big herds north to the Kansas railheads for several years. I'd take my pay and go down to El Paso, where my sister lived at the time, and buy a few cows and calves for myself. I kept doing that for several years until I had nearly a hundred head of my own. I was just twenty-one at the time.

"Anyway, as foolish as it sounds, I drove the whole works up the Rio Grande and west across the desert into the mountains of Arizona. That's where I built the ranch, increased the herd and all."

"And that's where you and Charley Imhoff fought the Apaches?" Davis queried.

"Yeah, that's it. Well, last March, a couple months after the big washout, I told you about . . . when Lisa and the baby died . . . cattle in that area began dying. I started finding them dropped dead in their tracks. The first week it hit my place I lost eight cows. I was getting worried. None of the old-timers around had seen anything like it.

"Then the second week I lost over a hundred head. There was so many I couldn't even drag them off the range into a canyon. During the first week in April, half my herd was dead, and there was no way to protect the rest. All up and down Surprise Creek carcasses were scattered about. You couldn't go anywhere without smelling decaying cows.

"I couldn't stand to see the rest go down so I took off to Prescott to try to find out what was happening. They had some government agents specializing in developing the cow business in Arizona. It took me two weeks, but I talked a handful of them into going out to the ranch and looking things over. By the time we got back, not one single cow was left standing. Several of the ranches next to me got hit hard, but none were wiped out."

Davis cleared his throat and rubbed his disheveled hair. "What in the world hit those cows?"

"Well, no one knew. One agent said I should burn all the buildings, vacate the ranch, and never come back. Another said if I didn't stay and keep making improvements, I'd lose the place. This one old boy said he thought it was the curse of Carlos De Palma-Revera."

"What's that?"

"I guess the ranch was at one time part of a Spanish land grant to this guy Palma-Revera. Story has it he was murdered, and his ghost rides the range."

"Nice guy, huh?"

"Yeah, the fourth agent said if we had two hard winters in a row, it should clean the disease out. He made the most sense. He said it was something washed down the creek in the topsoil. Since the creek cuts through my place, I got the worst of it. All I know is, by Easter I was out of business.

"I went down to Tombstone for the summer. Army hired me to scout out those Dragoon Mountains. Work played out in November, so I rode back to the ranch to take another look. But there wasn't anything for me there. When I got a telegraph from Charley Imhoff, I started up this way. It seemed as good a direction as any."

"So where will you head now?"

"Come spring, I'll go back to south Texas. I'll just cowboy along until I have enough of my own to start a little spread."

"You're not going to look for Charley's claim?" Davis asked.

Brannon looked over at the old prospector. "You think he really found gold?"

"Yep, I do."

"Well, I could postpone my return just a little," Brannon laughed and got up out of the tub.

In a few minutes, he was clean-shaven and dry, sitting on a bench up close to the fire.

"Everett, are you sure you don't want a bath? It's a shame to waste that water."

"A bath? It's unhealthy for a man my age. I'll go out to the hot springs when I really need one."

"I figure it's after midnight. What do you think?" Brannon asked.

Everett Davis struggled to sit up. "I guess you're right."

"Then it's Merry Christmas and time for some sleep."

"If you don't mind, Brannon, would you hand me that Bible you borrowed to bury that old boy last week."

"Now you aren't going to start getting religious on me, are you?"

"I never knowed I quit," Davis replied. "What's the matter, Brannon, you never spent any time reading the good book?"

"Never had much time. Oh, I suppose I've heard most all of it at one time or another," Brannon added. "It's kind of late now, isn't it?"

"Boy, it's Christmas. If you can't read about the baby Jesus and the angels and shepherds now, when can you? You just go on to sleep if you'd like, but I never get tired of hearing that story."

Everett Davis began to read out loud, and somewhere between Gabriel and the wise men, Brannon drifted into sleep.

The minute he opened his eyes the next morning, he sensed a good day coming. He stretched outside the cabin and surveyed the clear blue sky. The snow swelled about three feet high to clean and smoothe the rocky landscape. Clumped to the tall pines, it sparkled as pieces of ice slid off the limbs with an occasional gust of wind.

In the barn, Sage seemed anxious to eat for a change.

"It's Christmas, old boy, and I brought you some honey and oats."

Brannon exercised the horse by walking him around and around the wagon bed in the center of the barn. While leading the horse, he noticed what he thought was a pile of extra blankets in the corner of one of the empty stalls. He reached down to grab the top blanket.

Moments later, Stuart Brannon kicked open the front door of the cabin and swung a large bundle into the room.

"What on earth?" Davis sputtered.

"I found her in the barn, an Indian girl. She's been beat up bad and—"

Everett Davis dragged himself over to the table. "And what?"

"And she's very pregnant."

THREE

"Good heavens! Look at her face!" Davis gasped. "Grab that hot water off the fire, and I'll dig out some clean clothes I was saving 'til spring."

Stuart Brannon laid the girl in his bunk and covered her shivering body with a blanket. He moved quickly, almost instinctively. She had not opened her swollen eyes nor shown any sign of coming to.

He dipped a torn towel into the hot water and tried to wipe some of the dirt and blood off her face and out of her hair. Brannon kept mumbling, "Who would ever treat a woman like this? How could this happen?"

The air hung heavy in the cabin, yet he sensed a difference. A woman, any woman, changed the feeling of things.

"She can wear this wool shirt of mine." Everett Davis added, "It ain't too pretty, but it's clean and warm."

"Now how are we going to get it on her," Brannon quizzed, "her being passed out and all?"

The old man rubbed his beard. "Well, one of us will just have to pull off that soaking wet buckskin and slip this shirt on her, that's all."

"Good," Brannon nodded, "you do it." He rose, stepped away from the girl and turned his back.

"Me? Why me?" Davis protested.

"'Cause you're older, that's why."

"Yeah, but you were married once. You do it."

"It's not right. I can't do it. Don't make such a big deal out of it. You and I both know she'll catch pneumonia and die if we don't get that off her," Brannon insisted.

"Son, my back's hurting something terrible. I'd better crawl to my bunk and rest. You'll have to do it on your own."

"Davis, you coward! Get over here!"

"Sorry, Brannon, I just can't help. I'll close my eyes and you tell me when you're done."

Brannon sighed and looked again at the bloated and bruised face of the young girl on the bed. It looked to him as if she had sustained five or six hard blows. The more he looked and tried to clean, the madder he got.

"Honey, I don't know who you are, but nobody, I mean nobody should have to go through this," he spoke as he tried gently to pull back the long, black hair plastered in the dirt and blood on her face.

"You got her dressed decent yet?" Davis called out.

"Everett, I'm sorry, but I'm not changing this girl's clothes; that's all there is to it."

Suddenly, the girl's right eye, which was not swollen too bad, blinked open.

"Hand . . . me . . . the shirt," she whispered.

"Hey, you're awake! Everett, she's coming to!" Brannon shouted.

"I . . . have been . . . awake . . . the whole time." Each word was forced and labored.

"But why didn't you say . . . the whole time? You heard all the conversation?"

Her face showed no expression. Her open eye looked dull with pain. "I didn't know what kind of men you were. I was afraid you would also hurt me."

"Look, you won't get hurt here." Stuart Brannon continued, "But we've got to get you out of that wet buckskin. You are freezing."

"Hand me the shirt. I will change."

"Right. Sure. Here, wait!" Brannon jerked back the shirt. "Just a minute."

He crossed the cabin and pulled a dusty tarp down from the rafters. Grabbing the axe, he chopped a couple of short pieces off a rope. He then tied the tarp to the beam above the bunk. The tarp drooped down to the floor, making a partition between the girl's bunk and the rest of the cabin. "Here's the shirt, miss. Sorry we don't have a dress or a skirt or something."

"Could you please hand me a bowl of that hot water?"

"Sure, here, I'll just slide it under this tarp."

"May I use this small blanket for a skirt?" she asked, her voice gaining some strength.

"Oh, yeah, sure." Brannon went over by Everett Davis. Although the tarp hung in place, both men stared at the fire as they talked.

"You speak good English for a, you know, an Indian," Davis added.

"The father of this child is white," she added.

"So, you're married?" Brannon questioned.

"I am Nez Perce. When I was young, the Bannocks raided our camp and carried me off. Then they traded me to the Utes, and the Utes sold me to the white man for one horse. Is this what you mean by being married? Do you have any extra food? I am very hungry."

Brannon jumped up and grabbed a pan. Spooning in some beans, he handed it behind the tarp to the girl.

"Thank you. The white man I lived with was a bad man. He made me cook and clean his cabin and take care of his horses."

"That's all?" the old man asked.

"He made me do whatever he wanted of me," she spoke

softly. "But he began to beat me when he found out about the baby. He is in Tres Casas, but I ran away."

"Where are you going?"

"Idaho."

"In the winter?" Brannon continued the questions.

"I have relatives there."

"But you can't walk through these storms! You'll never make it."

"I have no choice but to try. I made it through the pass—barely."

"Then you stumbled through the woods to the barn?" Brannon probed.

"I do not know how I got to your barn. I am very tired. Do you have a comb?"

"Everett, have you got a comb?"

"Me? You're the fella that likes to dude up."

"Look, there's a comb around here someplace. I used it just the other day." Stuart Brannon stumbled around the cabin searching for a comb.

"Say, er, we don't know your name. Come to think of it, you don't know ours. I'm Stuart Brannon, and the old man is Everett Davis. The reason he can't move around much is that he has a bullet stuck in his back."

Brannon wiped the comb on his pants and then handed it around behind the tarp. It took a moment for him to realize that the girl was not taking the comb, nor was she speaking.

"Ma'am? Are you all right?"

Panicked, he took a quick glance behind the tarp.

"Is she dead?" Davis hollered out.

"No, just asleep." Brannon smiled. He laid the comb beside her bunk and returned to the fire.

"Kind of poetic, ain't it?" Everett sat on the edge of his bed.

"What's poetic about a beat-up girl?"

"I mean, this being Christmas and all. You know, a young

lady, laden with child and having no place to spend the night. Sort of like that first Christmas, right, Brannon?"

"Yeah, I guess. What are we going to do with her?"

The old man winced with a sharp pain and settled back down in his bunk. "If I get that thing caught wrong, the pain is fierce. The girl? Well, until spring thaw we can't do anything. Nobody can leave the cabin in this weather."

"That's what I was thinking. I'll give her my bunk. I never did fit it anyway. I'll bring in some extra straw and make a pallet over there behind the table. It's getting a bit crowded in here. Have you got enough food for another mouth?"

"Two mouths," Everett corrected. "It's a cinch she won't carry that baby much longer."

"Well, maybe we got time to figure that one out. I'm going out to check around a little. I don't want to find out someone was following her."

"Yeah, well, if you happen to see a Christmas goose, or a glazed ham, or a pie, you could bring it home. It might be nice to have something special for dinner."

Both men forced a laugh as Stuart Brannon shoved open the door and stepped out into the bright light reflected from snow.

At first, the air stung his face, but the clear blue sky and the clean rays of the sun made it seem more tolerable. With his right arm carrying his rifle across his shoulders and his left hand crammed into his coat pocket, Brannon hiked toward the frozen creek bed. The mountain on the other side of the icy draw was covered with snow-laden trees. He decided to climb high enough to look back down on the cabin and nearby terrain.

About halfway up the mountain, he came to a small clearing. He kicked the snow off a stump and sat down, surveying the cabin and creek below. Letting his eyes wander in circles around the cabin, he looked for signs of activity or movement. The only indication of life, besides the cabin and barn itself, was the snakelike column of smoke from the chimney. Everything else sat silent and still.

Strengthened by the quiet beauty of the scene, Brannon climbed to the top of the mountain and once again stopped to inspect. The far side of the mountain looked identical to the near side, minus the cabin and barn. Steep, tree-lined mountains, held captive by tons of snow, greeted his vision in every direction. Looking north, he spotted what looked like a small lake that was not frozen over.

"That must be Everett's hot springs," he mumbled out loud and crunched down the hill in that direction.

By the time he plowed down to the hot springs, his pant legs and boots were soaked and his feet rubbed cold and raw. After plunging his hands into the hot water, he plopped down and eased off his boots. Laying his rifle next to the boots, Brannon waded out into the middle of the stream and sat down on a large, dry boulder. The steam from the hot springs seemed to heat the air around him as well.

Some rare moments make harsh memories flee. Arizona faded to the distant past. Everett Davis and the Indian girl seemed far removed. Stuart Brannon couldn't help feeling good. He wiggled his toes and reached down to splash some of the warm mineral water on his face.

With water still dripping, he heard the distinctive crunch of someone, or something, breaking through the crust of snow. Without standing, he pulled his Colt from its holster and stared over at his rifle, twenty feet away.

The startled Indian leading the brown and white horse shouted something behind him and then reached toward his mount.

Brannon leveled his gun at the Indian and remained seated.

"I don't know if you understand what I'm saying, but if you bring a weapon off that horse, I'll have to shoot you!" he shouted.

The Indian didn't move, but he did glance down at Brannon's boots and rifle.

"Tell your friends to come out beside you."

The Indian stood expressionless.

Brannon slowly rose to his feet and cocked the hammer back on the pistol. "I said, tell them to come out!"

Turning his head slightly, the Indian called out, and instantly two others came into view leading their horses. Brannon waded carefully across the stream, never taking his aim away from the first Indian. He reached down and picked up his rifle with his left hand.

"Wait!" the Indian called out. "We only want water."

He motioned toward water bags draped across the horse. For the first time, Stuart Brannon noticed that all three Indians looked quite young, and indeed each had several water bags.

Without lowering his guns, Brannon nodded, "Go ahead, get your water."

All three hurried to the edge of the hot springs and filled the bags with water. *Everett had said something about a dozen or so Utes,* Brannon's mind flashed. He wanted to turn and survey the area, but he knew he couldn't relax his aim.

They finished loading the water bags on their horses without talking and then started to lead them away from the spring. Brannon holstered his pistol and raised his rifle into position.

The Indian who had spoken to him turned and waved. "We will meet again," he called, and then he spoke in Ute to the other two with him. All three Indians laughed as they led the horses into the woods and out of Brannon's sight.

He hurried to get his boots on, searching for a direction to exit the area undetected by the Indians. The leafless, snow-covered brush leading downstream from the springs offered the best cover, but it was in an opposite direction from the cabin. Knowing it was his best chance, Brannon pushed his way through the brush slowly, trying to make as little sound as possible.

Constantly looking back in the Indians' direction, he could see no sign of their return. But Brannon, by nature, could take no chances. He was fairly sure they would report the news to the others, and another band, better armed, would soon arrive.

As he crept downstream, he could tell by the increasing amount of ice forming along the stream bed that the hot springs were cooling off. In a particularly brushy portion of the creek, the clear water ended, and the ice stretched from bank to bank. He stopped quickly as he saw movement in the bushes ahead.

Out of the reeds, across the ice, and into the water waddled a large Canadian goose. Brannon almost laughed as he thought of Everett Davis's joke about Christmas dinner. The bird was so close and large, it would be a simple shot, yet he hesitated, not wanting to give away his escape route to the Indians.

Stuck in the dilemma, he stared at the goose as it paddled across the little stream. Two things Brannon hated: when other people tried to control his life and indecision.

Knowing his pistol made a little less noise than his rifle, he pulled it out of its holster and quickly shot the goose. The sound echoed and reechoed up the mountain slope, shattering the winter stillness. He grabbed the goose by the neck, tossed it over his shoulders, and stormed straight up the mountain.

If I can get high enough on the hill before they spot me, I can plan some sort of defense.

Halfway up the hill, he stopped to catch his breath. He scanned the hot springs and stream, but could see no signs of Indians following him. Relieved, he turned back towards the top and plowed on through the snow.

If they aren't following me, where are they? The cabin!

Brannon spotted the spiral of smoke from the fireplace, but could not yet see the cabin itself. He stumbled down through the snow, twice dropping the goose. Once he lost his footing and rolled head over heels.

He approached the cabin with caution, looking around for signs of visitors. The only tracks in the snow were those he had made himself. He stopped in front of the door, straining to hear any conversation inside. He shoved the door open and stepped in.

"You been out there playing in the snow?" Everett laughed.

"Is everything all right here? You had any visitors?"

The old man sat at the table carving on a stick with a large hunting knife. "Visitors? Nope. Why do you ask?"

"I ran into some Utes up by the hot springs. I thought maybe they circled around to here."

"How many?"

"I only saw three, but they were gathering water for at least six to ten."

"I would have figured they would be down in the low country by now. The pass must have snowed them in too."

Brannon banged the big goose down on the table. "So everything is all right? Well, we're going to have our Christmas dinner after all."

"I didn't say everything is all right," Davis replied with a glance toward the tarp that divided the cabin. "I just said we had no more visitors."

"So—what's wrong?"

"Elizabeth woke up and informed me that she's about to have her baby."

"Elizabeth?"

"She's only eighteen years old, you know."

"Have the baby?" Brannon replied wildly. "You mean—soon?"

"She said today."

"Today?"

"Any minute."

"I thought we had a few weeks."

"She said the rough treatment brought it on."

Brannon took off his gun holster and hung it on the wall. "What are we supposed to do?"

"You tell me," Davis cracked.

"Everett, I can't do this again. I told you what happened last time."

"Well, it's a cinch an old, crippled-up fellow like myself won't be of any help. Go talk to her. Maybe she has some suggestions."

Brannon spun on his heels and stomped over to the partition.

"Eh, ma'am? Elizabeth? Are you all right?"

There was a slight pause; then with difficulty, she answered, "Yes, Mr. Brannon."

"Look, I want to be real honest. The two of us probably won't be of much help to you. I mean, we just don't know what to do."

"Mr. Brannon," she spoke softly and slowly, "why do you always stay behind the curtain when you speak to me? Are you ashamed to look at my face?"

Stuart Brannon edged around the curtain and peered down at Elizabeth. Her long, black hair was combed straight, but all he could see were the bruises and swellings. His face reddened with shame—shame that a man had actually done that to her. Ashamed that she was forced to go through this experience in a frozen stage stop with a couple of helpless drifters looking on.

"Have you been through this before?" he finally asked.

"What?"

He cleared his throat, "I mean, have you had children before?"

"No."

Once again he looked away from her. "Well, you'll do fine. I'm sure your mother told you all about it, right?"

"I was taken from my family at an early age."

The sweat started to bead up on Brannon's forehead and cheeks. He rubbed them with his right hand.

"But you know what to do, right?" He shifted his weight from one foot to the other.

Now, it was Elizabeth who looked away. She stared at the wall. "Mr. Brannon, I am very scared. I am afraid that when he hit me, he hurt my baby, I am afraid that I will have a difficult time."

Brannon wheeled back across the room towards Davis. His words came out in measured disgust.

"Everett, this is exactly what I told you I can't handle. One man can't take that much pain. It took me one whole year to ever talk about my Lisa, and now, now . . . I just can't sit at the bedside of another dying woman, do you hear me! I won't do it! I can't do it!"

He stomped across the floor towards the door of the cabin. Instinctively he grabbed up his rifle and walked out into the afternoon sunlight. The contrasts overwhelmed him. Outside, the world looked so peaceful, quiet, perfect. The sun still high, the sky still blue, the snow glistening as it hung heavy on the pines, firs, and spruces. But inside, the cabin painted a scene of smoky dark pain and turmoil. He dropped his back against the barn. For a minute he clutched his arms tight against his stomach, trying to relieve the horrible deep ache.

This is crazy! I shouldn't even be here. I'm supposed to be down in Arizona trying to make something of that ranch. And what's she doing here? How in the world did she find this barn in last night's snowstorm? I'm no woman doctor. I'm not even a cow doctor. Everything I try to take care of ups and dies on me.

He yanked off his hat and ran his fingers through his hair. Taking big, deep breaths of cold air, he tried to sort things out.

I could just saddle up old Sage and ride out of here. Maybe the good weather would hold up 'til I made it through the pass. I sure can't run a hospital.

He stomped into the barn searching for a few empty feed sacks. He stuffed them with hay from the loft.

Indians have just got to take care of Indians. These kinds of things probably are happening all over, and I can't be responsible. She doesn't have any right to shove this on me.

He tossed the full sacks to the floor below and climbed down the ladder, still mumbling to himself.

Eighteen years old and she doesn't know what to do? What has she been thinking about for the past nine months? Surely she asked somebody!

Jamming two big sacks of straw under each arm, he shoved the barn door open with his shoulder and tramped the fresh snow back around to the cabin.

"God help us," he muttered out loud as he pushed open the door. "Everett, we're going to have to use your bed. That little bunk is too narrow."

"I reckon you're right. What do you have that straw for?"

"For a clean, soft mattress. You, being laid up yourself, won't be of much help carrying her, so if you'll scoot yourself to the back side of the table, I'll get her over here closer to the fire."

Stuart Brannon began to operate on sheer will power. There was no time to think things through, no time to reflect, and no value to be gained by either. They would either survive or be destroyed by this, and at this point there was no alternative but to press on.

Brannon was surprised how light Elizabeth was. He guessed her weight to be less than one hundred pounds. She tried to smile, but it only hurt. She did look more comfortable in the larger bed.

"Elizabeth, if you've got any ideas, just shout them out."

"Brannon, what do you want me to do?" Everett broke in.

"Do you think you can hobble out to the barn?"

"I think so."

"Well, how about dressing out this goose? We still need a Christmas dinner," Brannon suggested.

Everett Davis limped toward the barn, dragging the goose behind him. "You holler at me if you need me," he called.

Stuart Brannon ripped down the tarp around the little bunk and hung it straight away from the fireplace, dividing the room in half. He picked up some food cans, clothing, and wood chips scattered around the floor on Elizabeth's side of the room.

"I can't find anything that looks like a baby bed. Do you think you'll have room in there?"

"It will be fine. I'm sorry for the trouble I've caused."

"Listen, I know I sounded harsh, it's just—"

"We will leave in a few days. When the baby gets strong enough."

"Leave? Where to?"

"We will go to my people."

"The Utes?"

"The Nez Perce."

"I told you that you can't walk to Idaho Territory in the middle of the winter!"

"It is Oregon . . . and we can do it."

"No, you can't. I won't let you go."

"You will force me to stay here?"

Brannon was stung by the word *force*. He sighed deeply and sat down on the bench next to the table. Once again he was talking to her through the tarp.

"Listen, I do not know who you are. I do not know

whether you are good or evil, whether you tell the truth or lie. And you do not know me. You have no idea whether I am a good man or a bad man—"

"I know you are good," she interrupted. "I see it in your eyes."

"And I see nothing but pain in yours," he added quickly, then bit his tongue. After a moment he continued, "But I won't force you to do anything. I don't want you to try to walk out of these mountains carrying a newborn baby. I would ask you to stay out the winter and find your way home in the spring."

"You ask me to stay with you?"

"Yes, I ask you."

"Then I will stay. But only until the flowers bloom."

"Good. Would you like some water to drink?"

"Yes, my mouth is very dry. How did you know?"

"It's a long story, and you don't want to hear it now."

Brannon carried over a cup of water. She rose up on one elbow and nodded her thanks. After a few sips, she asked, "Do you have a looking glass?

"You don't want to see."

"Is it bad?"

"Yes. But I'm sure it will heal."

"I used to be pretty when I was young."

"You are still young, and I'm sure you are pretty."

"Today I feel very old and ugly."

"Well, a baby will make you happy."

"Yes, and I want a son. Life is too difficult for an Indian girl."

"Things will look better after winter is over. Do you need anything else?"

"If I am going to stay, I will clean the house and cook."

"Now wait a minute," he protested.

"Mr. Brannon, I will clean and cook. This room is messy, and it smells bad."

Stuart Brannon sat staring at the fire. There was just nothing left to say. Finally he added another log to the fire.

He stepped outside the door again. The sun was down behind the trees, and the crisp air stung his lungs as he inhaled.

Elizabeth let out a piercing yell. He raced back into the cabin.

"It is time," she panted.

"Right. Now, what do you want—"

"It is time," she repeated, "for you to leave."

"What?"

"Mr. Brannon, I would like to be alone."

"Alone? Are you sure? I thought you were scared."

"I am very frightened. But I want to be alone."

"Oh, yeah, well, sure. Look, I'll be out on the porch."

Stuart Brannon did not wait for an answer. He slipped out to the front porch and caught sight of Everett Davis looking out through the barn door. Both men stared across the snow at each other as the girl's shrieks grew in volume and intensity.

Suddenly, the wails stopped. Brannon grabbed for the door, hesitated, then knocked.

"Elizabeth! Elizabeth? Are you all right?"

He heard nothing except for Everett Davis shuffling through the snow behind him.

FOUR

"Is she all right?" wheezed Everett Davis as he held his right side.

Stuart Brannon stuck his head in the cabin door and called out, "Elizabeth? Elizabeth?"

The two men listened at the door.

Finally, they heard a startled cry from a voice much younger than Elizabeth's.

Again Brannon called, "Are you all right? Is everything square?"

"I am tired. It is over."

Brannon took one step inside the room, "Over? You mean the baby's born, and everything?"

"Yes, but I need some time alone—to clean up," she said, pausing between the baby's cries to catch her breath.

"Oh, yeah, look, we're right outside the door. You yell for us if you need anything."

"I have yelled enough for one day," came the reply.

Both men stumbled back outside and closed the door. Then Brannon stuck his head back inside. "Elizabeth? Say, did you get your boy?"

"Yes . . . he is beautiful. His name shall be Littlefoot."

The men rammed into each other as they backed out of the doorway.

"It's a boy, Stuart Brannon, and his name is Littlefoot!" Everett Davis hollered as if Brannon were far away.

Then Brannon braved the door one more time. "Oh, excuse me, Elizabeth? The boy . . . Is he, you know, healthy?"

"Oh, yes. His hands, his feet, his ears—everything is perfect."

"Uh, I don't hear him crying now."

"He is too busy to cry."

"Busy?"

"He's having his supper."

"Supper? Oh. Yeah. Sure. Listen, take your time. Me and Everett will be out next to the barn roasting that goose over the fire. Come on, Davis. Littlefoot's eating supper."

"Well, ain't that something. You and me stuck up here on Christmas, and the Lord sends us a young lady and a baby. Almost prophetic, don't you think?"

Brannon gathered some logs from behind the barn and started building a fire out next to the corral. "Everett, it's a coincidence, but I don't see anything religious in it."

"Son, are you fighting God?"

"What are you talking about?"

"Last night, you got short with me when I read the Bible. Tonight, I mention a baby born on Christmas, and you stove-up again. Sounds to me like you got an argument with the Almighty."

"Everett, me and God have an understanding. I don't bother Him for anything, and He doesn't bother me. Go get that goose. It'll take two hours to roast it good."

The evening temperature dipped, but the men huddled close to the coals of the low fire. They faced the fire for a while, then turned their backs to it. Neither spoke much.

Everett Davis cleared his throat. "Brannon, I still say it's a special treat to have a baby born. New life . . . another generation . . . a little bundle of activity."

Brannon gazed off into the stillness of a dark winter night. "Did you ever think about what kind of life that kid will have? A half-breed with no father, no home, no tribe. You really think there'll be any Indians left twenty-five years from now? Born into poverty, misery, it's a dead-end street. The kid will never live to be an old man."

"Man, what is eating at you? First you're scared to death the baby won't make it. Now you act like you wished it didn't," Davis postured.

"Everett, I want to know why."

"Why?"

"Why on God's earth did that baby in that shack of a cabin live and my baby die? Why did that poor abandoned, beat-up, half-starved, and mostly frozen Indian girl come through all of this? And why did my Lisa, in the center of love and comfort and family . . . die? I want to know why. Tell me why, Everett."

Brannon turned back to the fire and added another log. "Don't get me wrong. I'm not angry at Elizabeth. I'm not mad at that baby. I've just got to know why! Is it God that sits in the heavens choosing which babies live and which ones die? Well, I don't like His choice. I want to know what the system is for selection, 'cause it just doesn't make any sense to me."

Everett Davis coughed, then paused before answering. "If you think I'm supposed to have an answer for that, I'm afraid I'll disappoint you. I just don't know why. There are times this whole world seems out of kilter. During the war, I went back home and signed up with the Twenty-fourth Michigan. We marched into the battle at Gettysburg and eight out of ten of us were shot down. To this day, I don't understand why I hiked out without a scratch. I just don't know why I lived but Hershel Briggens, running about three steps to the right of me, took four shots in the head and died before he hit the ground. But I figure me being ignorant of such things doesn't make God any the less."

"Well, Everett, that might work for you, but it still tastes sour in my mouth," Brannon replied.

Both men once again stared at the coals in silence.

Brannon was poking at the roasting goose to see if it was done when Elizabeth called, "Mr. Brannon! Mr. Davis! Please come in out of the cold."

"Everett, don't let on to Elizabeth what I was saying. And don't be harpin' on me about religion. Each man's got to work that out for himself, and I haven't got there. That's all."

"You carry in that goose," Everett added, "and I'll give Sage some hay. See you in the cabin."

Brannon carried the bird, still skewered on a pole, toward the cabin. "Hey, have we got some more of those canned peaches or tomatoes? We ought to do this up right."

"Under my bunk against the wall. There's a quart of cherries," Davis grinned.

"Cherries? You've been hiding a jar of cherries?" Brannon laughed.

"No, I ain't hiding them. I'm saving them for something special—like Christmas."

"And babies?"

"Right, for little babies. Go on, I'll be right there."

Any hostility Stuart Brannon may have possessed against the baby disappeared the second he laid eyes on its little face and black shock of hair.

"He's a jewel," Brannon boasted, "and he's as handsome as his mother!"

"His mother is very, very tired. I think perhaps we should go to sleep now." She shuffled to the bed, carrying the little blanket-wrapped bundle in her arms.

"He really does look like you." Brannon followed behind.

"I am glad he does not look like his father. He will be raised Indian. He will be a brave warrior."

"Listen, do you want something to eat? We roasted the goose, and we've got some bread and beans and—cherries! Everett has a whole quart of cherries." Brannon stuck his arm under the bed and pulled out the dust-covered jar.

"I am very hungry. I will try to stay awake." Elizabeth sat on the edge of the bed rocking back and forth with the baby in her arms.

"You sit right there. I'll slice off some of this bird. Here's a pan, and some bread, and of course the cherries. Here's the whole jar; just pour out what you want."

"Mr. Brannon." Elizabeth glanced over at the food, then at the baby. Still bruised and battered, she smiled. "Merry Christmas."

"Merry Christmas to you, Elizabeth. I'm very sorry we have no present to give to your baby."

"You have given me much in one day. You have provided food, warmth, and a place for me and my baby to spend the winter. I will not soon forget such kindness."

"You go ahead and eat. I'm going to step out and see what's taking Everett so long. Old Sage must be giving him a bad time."

Stuart Brannon took a stick from the fire and lit the oil lantern. It produced no more than a dull glow, but that was enough to see his way to the barn. It was completely dark inside.

"Everett? Everett! Where are you?" Brannon drew his pistol by instinct and searched the shadows. He heard groaning from the base of the ladder to the loft and rushed around the wagon to find Davis lying flat on his back.

"Everett! What happened?" Brannon holstered his gun and set the lantern on the wagon. Bending down, he lifted up Davis's head.

"I tried to climb to the loft. I must have slipped, but I

landed on my back." He choked out each word. "That bullet must have shifted . . . the pain . . . I ain't never had such pain. I can't move nothin'."

Davis's body lay perfectly still. Almost restful. Even his face showed little expression. Like it was frozen. But his eyes. Brannon thought his eyes cried out with hurt and fear.

"Look, I've got to get you back in that cabin where it's warm. I can't pick you up like that Indian girl, and I'm not sure how to move you at all."

Brannon stood up and searched wildly with his eyes around the shadows of the barn wall. "Look, I'll grab some of those barn boards and slide you over to the cabin."

Again expressionless, Everett labored, "You won't slide me down the hill with that horse, will you?"

Their conversation belittled the fear they both felt.

"You're not going to use this fall as an excuse to get an extra helping of cherries." Brannon spoke the words flatly. He laid two of the barn boards down next to Everett Davis. It took four tries to get him over on the boards with a minimum amount of pain. Then Brannon lifted up the boards at Davis's head and started dragging the board like an Indian travois through the barn door and to the cabin.

With great effort, he shoved open the door and dragged Davis to the narrow bunk. Finally, by getting on his knees, he lifted up board and body and slid them onto the bed.

"Elizabeth, Everett's really hurt bad and—" Brannon stopped talking when he peeked around the tarp and saw that Elizabeth and the baby were sleeping. He picked her plate off the floor. The jar of cherries was empty.

Brannon pulled a bench over by Davis's bunk and tried to talk.

"Everett, can you eat? I can feed you some bread and meat, or something."

"Pain . . . it just won't stop. No food, not yet."

"Look, I'm going to sit right here," Brannon insisted. "If you need something, let me know. You want a drink?"

"My lips . . . on fire . . . "

Brannon grabbed a rag and dipped it in the water. Then he wiped the sweat off his friend's forehead and laid the damp rag on his lips. Davis closed his haunted eyes, and Brannon reached down and gripped his work-callused hand. It lay limp.

Listening to Davis's heavy breathing, Brannon scraped up some food in a pan and sat back down next to Everett Davis. The roasted goose and the bread had no taste in his mouth, but he ate them anyway.

Merry Christmas? Is this really Christmas? Here I am cooped up like a nurse in a hospital. Is this the way Christmas is supposed to be spent? Maybe so, maybe so.

Stuart Brannon was a man of action. He could punch cattle, build barns, dig for water, hunt elk, and fight Indians if he had to. But he didn't much like sitting around watching other people hurt. And he didn't like being indecisive.

He physically ached as he sat next to Everett Davis all night trying to decide what to do next. It seemed he should try to get to town and get a doctor. But it would take nearly two weeks to get through the snow and back again—if he made it at all.

Then he couldn't go because all three people in the cabin needed him here to take care of them.

Maybe I should load them all up on a sled and take the whole works with me, but that little warrior would freeze out in the cold.

Back and forth it went as he tended the fire, checked on the occasionally crying baby, and sat at the bench by Davis. At best he was able to get Everett to drink a little water, but he never got him to eat.

About daylight, Brannon went out to bring in more wood and to exercise Sage. A mass of black, heavy clouds hung about on the tops of the trees, and he knew a snowstorm would soon start. He fed his horse extra hay and made several trips to the woodshed just in case they would be cabin-bound.

There's no way anyone can head out in a storm.

When he finished stirring the fire, he was surprised to turn and see Elizabeth sitting up on the edge of the bed, holding the baby. "Oh, morning, you two. Did I wake you up?"

"Oh, we have been awake much of the night. Did you sleep?"

"No, er, Everett fell in the barn last night and can't move. A few weeks ago, he was back-shot, and the bullet is still in there."

"Can't you remove it?"

"It's just too deep. It must be next to the spine. I've got to get him to a doctor, and what with a big storm blowing in, it doesn't look good."

"I watched a doctor in Tres Casas remove a bullet from Mr. Rutherford. It was just like that."

"Rutherford? One of the Rutherford brothers? Do you know him?"

"He is the father of my child."

"Rutherford beat you up?"

Turning her eyes away from Brannon, she looked to the floor. "Yes."

"They shot a friend of mine."

"They shoot a lot of people."

"This guy was named Charley Imhoff. Did you know about him?"

"Yes, one of the gang killed him."

"Did you see it?"

"Oh, no, I was locked in the barn."

"Locked up?"

"When they left me, they would always tie me up and lock me in the barn. They were afraid I would try to run away again. But I heard them tell about killing your friend because he would not tell them where his gold was."

"Looks like I ought to meet this gang." Brannon gazed once again at the bruises on Elizabeth's face.

"They are very evil men. They think only of themselves."

Somehow those words caught Stuart Brannon by surprise. Of course, men like the Rutherfords were evil, but her definition of evil as being a person who thinks only of himself—Brannon knew that could often apply to him, too.

"You tried to run away, I take it. Often?"

"Yes, at first. But each time he would beat me more."

"How did you escape this time?"

"I think he wanted me gone. I was no longer of any value to him."

"Well, I guess Rutherford survived having the bullet cut out?"

"Yes, but it took several weeks to gain his strength back, and he is a very healthy man."

"And I'm no doctor. Everett will just have to pull through. We don't have any other choice."

"Would you please take care of Littlefoot for a moment?"

"Oh, no, ma'am, er, Elizabeth. Really, he's a beautiful little one, but I'm not too confident with babies. I'd be afraid of, you know—"

"Mr. Brannon, I must step out and take care of some things. Could you watch him for a moment then?"

"Oh, sure, I'll watch."

Elizabeth left the cabin, wrapped tightly in a blanket from the bed. Brannon went over and looked at the baby more closely. His tiny brown fingers seemed so perfect, miniature, and detailed. His little eyes were a dark, dark brown, almost black. They seemed to be alert. And the hair. He had never seen a newborn with so much hair. He reached down and put one of his fingers in the palm of the baby's hand. Littlefoot clutched tightly. "Well, little buckaroo, I hope you don't find too harsh of a world waiting for you."

Suddenly, Everett Davis cried out. Brannon hurried to his side.

"Everett? Can I get you something?"

The older man gazed at the rafters and didn't try to speak. His lips looked chapped and swollen, his forehead fevered. The baby began to cry in response to the old man's groans.

"Everett, she calls him Littlefoot. I've never seen a cuter little warrior."

The man in the bunk closed his eyes and didn't respond. Brannon took the rag and wiped Davis's forehead. He hadn't noticed Elizabeth standing by.

"How is he?"

Stuart Brannon turned and walked with Elizabeth back to her bed. "Not well. He just can't last long in this condition."

"You will have to cut the bullet out."

"It would kill him!"

"He is dying," she spoke quietly.

"I saw him work through this once before; maybe the bullet will shift."

"Do you believe that?"

"No." Brannon hung his hat on a peg in the wall and adjusted the wick on the lantern.

"Neither do I."

There were times when Stuart Brannon loved the ice cold purity of a snowy winter day. This was not one of those times. *At least in Arizona you've got a chance at finding a doctor. Up here a guy's absolutely stuck.* He walked back over to Davis's bed.

"Now listen, partner, don't you give up on me. We've got a baby to raise this winter, and I'm not going to play daddy without your help. As soon as this new storm blows out of here, we'll all sled down to Tres Casas, and I'll get some old doc to patch you up, you hear?"

Everett Davis lay motionless. He made no response to Brannon's words.

Stuart Brannon laid his head back on the wooden bench and closed his eyes. It had been such a long Christmas.

April was his favorite time to ride the mountains of Arizona. The desert bloomed, the calves pranced, the cows were content, and blazing sun splashed warmth across their faces. Lisa always rode with him that first spring. Never side-saddle, never on some old broken-down pony. She'd pick the tallest, fastest horse he would let her ride, and she'd gallop alongside of him for miles.

"My mother would die if she saw me doing this," Lisa would laugh. "'Now, little sister,' she would say, 'you must, at all times act like a lady, a Nash lady.'"

And that she could. Half the men in town went to church just to see Lisa Nash dressed in her Sunday best. "What in the world do you see in that guy, Brannon?" friends would tease her.

"Oh, he'll be the governor someday," she would smile and nod.

She had a knack of making him want to do his best. Brannon truly believed that he could do anything she wanted him to.

"Mr. Brannon."

Wait! Where are the blooming cactus? Where's Lisa? The cattle?

"Mr. Brannon!"

The cattle are all dead? What happened?

"Mr. Brannon. Wake up! Mr. Davis is calling you. He is very sick."

Stuart Brannon sat up quickly on the hard wooden bench and rubbed his eyes.

"Was I asleep?"

"Yes, for a long time. I think Mr. Davis is getting worse. He has been talking about a place called Gettysburg. Is that his home?"

Brannon stood up and stretched. Then he plunged his hands into the water bowl and splashed his face. Letting the water drip to his shirt, he went back to see Everett Davis.

Holding his friend's shoulder, he spoke softly, "Everett? Hey, it's me, Brannon."

The pained eyes opened and rolled to the side. "Read . . . " He coughed up the words. "Read to me."

"Read? Read what? The Bible?" Brannon stammered.

"Every . . . should . . . have . . . read . . . over . . . him."

Stuart Brannon hunted through the cabin and located Davis's little black Bible.

"Now, here goes. Listen, I'm not too good at reading out loud, so you'll have to put up with me." Brannon flipped through the pages, and then turned to Elizabeth who sat holding the baby on the other side of the table. "I don't even know where to begin."

He no longer noticed her bruised face, but looked right into her eyes.

"Start with the one called Matthew. A woman read it to me when I was a very little girl in Idaho. I would like to hear it again. I believe it was a very nice story," Elizabeth added.

Brannon cleared his throat and began to read. Once he began, he didn't know where to stop. But he didn't know what to say to Davis, so he kept reading. Elizabeth and the baby went back to lie down, and he read and read until he finished Matthew.

"Everett, I've got to get some chores done, can I—"

Suddenly he grabbed Davis's arm and felt for a pulse. Then he slammed his ear against the old man's chest listening for a heartbeat.

"Elizabeth, are you awake?"

"We are both awake."

"Look, Everett's about gone. I don't think he's coming to unless I get that bullet out of there."

"You are going to try it?"

"I have to. Do you have the stomach for watching me? Perhaps you can remember what that doctor did."

"I will watch. You will need to heat your knives."

"Yeah, I know that much. Can you lay the baby down and help me roll him over?"

For the next several minutes, they worked quickly without speaking. Brannon heated the two knife blades, and Elizabeth tore up some shirts into rags. He brought a pan of water close to the bed.

"I'm going to need the lantern held over here," he stated.

She came closer, holding the oil lamp with one hand and the baby with the other. "You must work quickly. He will lose much blood."

"Are you sure you can handle this?" He looked up at the young mother, with her still-battered face. She didn't need to answer his question.

The only good thing about it was that Davis was out, and Stuart Brannon did not have to think about the pain his knife was causing. Though the neglected fire was dimming, Brannon sweated profusely as he sliced his way deeper into Everett Davis's back. Littlefoot slept peacefully at his mother's side as she stood close by.

Brannon reached the upper edge of the exploded lead bullet and hoped to be able to flip it out with a heated knife. But the bullet was lodged tight. He knew he would have to reach in and pull on the bullet. He glanced down at his rough, blood-covered hands.

"Elizabeth. There it is! But I can't get it out. Can you, I mean, your hands are much cleaner . . . could you try to unlodge it and raise it out of there?"

"Hold the lantern. I will try."

Brannon stood and stretched his aching back as he held

the lantern. Elizabeth, with baby still in hand, took a deep breath and reached inside the man. Holding one end of the bullet, she rotated it around very slowly until it came free.

She turned to Brannon, "There! It is out."

He carried the lantern to the far side of the room searching through the shelves. "We've got to find something to sear that and keep if from infecting. Has he got any alcohol around here?"

"There is vinegar under my bed," she offered.

"Vinegar? That might work. What else is under there?"

"A picture of a beautiful lady and a can of tomatoes," she replied.

When they finished wrapping and tying a bandage around Everett Davis, Brannon and the girl cleaned up the room without speaking at all.

Brannon watched her move about the cabin. *She's a hard worker. We've been together a little over a day, and she feels like one of the family.*

After eating leftovers from the previous night, Elizabeth lay down.

"You should get some rest, too."

"I'll be all right, thanks."

"You will stay up all night, I think," she spoke softly.

"He will probably have a high fever. He will need to be cooled down."

"Yes," she added, "I know."

Brannon spent the night keeping wet rags on Everett Davis's forehead, nodding off to sleep at the table. His wife, Lisa, dominated every dream, and he hated to keep waking up.

By daylight, Davis had made no signs of coming to. His pulse seemed no stronger, but also no weaker.

Elizabeth stirred the fire with one hand and started cooking something for breakfast.

"I'm going to check on Sage." Brannon spoke for the first

time since the night before. He reached for his hat and his holster.

Snow from the previous night packed against the door. He had to kick the bottom of the door in order to get it open. The storm was wet and heavy and still hung on the treetops. He lit the lamp in the barn and tossed down some hay for Sage. Still in the loft, he lay back against the piles of hay and closed his eyes.

This time, he did not dream.

"Mr. Brannon!"

He pulled his gun from the holster and jumped to his feet when he heard Elizabeth's scream. The lantern had gone out, and the barn was almost dark. He fumbled his way down the ladder and across the barn, shoving open the door. A heavy snowstorm raged, and it was so dark he could not even guess the time of day.

Still carrying his drawn pistols, he violently pushed open the door and stomped inside. Two men, looking half-frozen, stood, hands raised and speechless. With Everett Davis's buffalo gun propped against the table and Littlefoot cradled in her left arm, Elizabeth nervously held the men hostage.

FIVE

"Well, boys, is this a social call, or are you just out on a pleasure ride?" Brannon looked them over good. The taller one wore a black bowler tied down around his ears with a dirty bandana. The other one had a long, drooping mustache and a wide-brimmed hat pulled low on his head. "Who are you and what do you want?" he barked.

"I see you're an American, thank heavens." The taller man tried to smile. "I'm Edwin Fletcher. English, you know. And this is Henri Trudeaux. He's French. Doesn't speak a word of English."

"Elizabeth, what's going on here?" Brannon asked.

"I was asleep with Littlefoot when I heard noises in the cabin. I thought it was you. The short one came around the corner and yelled something I didn't understand, so I grabbed the gun off the wall."

"My word, she speaks English." Fletcher lowered his hands slightly.

"Keep them high, mister." Brannon ordered. "Let me repeat, what are you doing here and what do you want?"

"If we might lower our hands a bit. We are freezing. May we move closer to the fire?"

Brannon signaled to them with his pistol. The Englishman

spoke in French to the other man. Then both hunkered down next to the fireplace.

"I'm sorry if I offended your wife, sir. We have been walking through the snow for two days, and frankly we had given up hope of finding help," Fletcher offered.

"First, she is not my wife . . . "

Trudeaux spoke to Fletcher. "He asks why you have beaten the young lady."

"Beaten her?" Brannon cocked the pistol at the now-cowering Frenchman.

"Please wait!" Fletcher spoke rapidly. "We are new to this country. We have heard of the wild savages, and when we saw how she looked, we were afraid she would shoot us. I implore you, we need your help."

Brannon sat down at the table and laid his pistol between his right hand and the two squatting men. "What kind of help do you need?"

"Sir, we left Tres Casas three weeks ago. There was a warm wind blowing, and we were told we could make it up to the Little Yellowjacket. We are going to look for gold. But the storms hit us right as we reached the pass, and we used up all our supplies waiting it out. About five days ago, our horses were chased off in a skirmish with some hostiles, so, as you can see, we are desperate. Many of us couldn't walk any farther, so Henri and I decided to push on and and try to find help."

"Others? There are more of you?"

"Oh yes. Twelve of us, all together. Tristo Lanier is the man leading the group. Do you know him?"

"Never heard of him."

"Then there is Miles and McHenry. Miles was shot by some Indians and is in bad shape. Red Hapner and a fellow called Skeet started back to Tres Casas to find help, and then there's the Mulroneys. Irish—poor folks, with three sick children. That's why we need help. We've got to get them out of that pass to safety."

"Kids? You brought kids out into these mountains in the winter?" Brannon pressed.

"Look, they aren't ours. But you know, talk has it in Tres Casas that the first two dozen folks to make it to the Little Yellowjacket will make all the money. We plan to be in that group." Fletcher stood and looked around. "Listen, do you happen to have any soup or bread or anything?"

"Here, help yourself." Brannon took a pot of soup off the fire and placed bread on the table.

"Did you say it took you two days to reach here from the pass?"

"Yes, but I have no idea how much time we wasted wandering around in circles. The storm was so heavy at the pass I don't even know if we can find our way back. Do you know how to get there from here?"

Brannon brushed the question aside. "What are the children's names?"

"I beg your pardon?"

"I said, what are the kids' names?"

"Er, Sean, Stephen, and Sarah. Why?" Fletcher looked up from his bowl of soup.

"How old are they?"

"Well, six, five, and four, I believe. But why?"

"Describe Mrs. Mulroney."

"Oh, she's about five feet tall. Coal-black hair, like this young lady. But of course she's as white as cow's milk. Do you know her?"

"No."

"It will be dark soon. Should we leave for the pass?"

"Perhaps in the morning. You men can sleep in the barn."

Fletcher nodded. "Certainly. Thank you very much." He then spoke to the Frenchman for several minutes as they finished their food.

Brannon walked with them out to the barn.

"Oh, good! You have a horse!" Fletcher pointed to Sage.

"Yeah, and the last man who took him without asking is buried right outside the barn. Is that clear?"

Brannon re-lit the lantern for the men and returned to the cabin.

"Are those men telling the truth?" Elizabeth asked.

"That's what I've been wondering. They looked honest."

"But no one would actually try to take a family through this weather," she cautioned.

"That's what sounds strange. Maybe they're trying to get us out of the cabin . . . or, at least, find out who is in here."

Brannon walked over to Everett Davis's bunk.

"How is Mr. Davis?" Elizabeth asked.

"He's still unconscious, but I think the bleeding is slowing down. Elizabeth, if I go with these men, will you be all right? I mean, are you strong enough?"

"I will be fine. But I will not be of much help to Mr. Davis. I could not lift him or anything."

"If the weather permits, I think we could reach the others by tomorrow night and be back the following day."

"If it is not an ambush."

Stuart Brannon slept very little that night. He walked the floor, added wood to the fire, checked on Everett Davis, looked in on Littlefoot and his mother, and started the routine again. By daylight he had roused the men out of the barn, made several barn-board sleds, and gathered up a sack of food for them to carry.

Finally, he went back into the cabin to talk to Elizabeth. "If there are women and children out there, I must go. It's my duty."

"Duty to who?"

"To . . . decency . . . to mankind, you know . . . to God. Anyway, Everett will understand."

"Mr. Brannon, does your God inspire you to do things for other people even if they are dangerous?"

"My God? No, it's the old man here who's religious. It's just—"

"I heard you reading the book for most of the night," she added.

"Well, that was Everett's idea. Not that I see anything wrong with it, mind you."

"I believe a God who inspires a person to do good to others without thinking of himself is a very good God. When you come back, will you read to me some of the book?"

"The old man is the reader. He knows it all by heart. Listen, Everett will either get better, in which case try to get him to eat, or he'll get worse, in which case I'll bury him when I return. And I will return."

"Yes, I believe you will, Mr. Brannon."

The three men left the cabin right after the sun came up. Brannon insisted the other men lead the way so he could keep an eye on them. He would snap a command through the storm, and they would go to the right or left. Each of the three pulled a small, empty sled through the snow.

The snowstorm came in spurts, but visibility was never much higher than the trees. Brannon had hoped to sight in on the mountains in order to find Brighton Pass. Now he would have to trust memory and instinct.

At noon, they found a large, sprawling red fir tree that provided dry shelter underneath. They huddled together and ate some of the provisions.

"You don't trust us very well, Mr. Brannon," Fletcher spoke softly as he retied the bandana around his hat.

"I don't know you very well. Should I trust you?"

Every sentence was then translated into French for Trudeaux.

"Is everyone in the West so suspicious?"

"Only those who plan on a long life. Mr. Fletcher, the

closer you get to gold country, the crazier folks become. Some quiet grocery store clerk from Philadelphia becomes a raving killer if someone moves in on his claim. Tell me about yourself. How long have you been in the States?"

"Oh, for only a month. I sailed from Liverpool to the West Indies, then around the horn to San Diego. From there I took the overland to Prescott, bought a horse, and rode to Tres Casas. That's where I met Henri."

"Must have cost you a fortune to sail around the cape."

"Actually, money is the least of my worries. We have a family business that makes more than my five brothers and I can spend."

"So what in the world is the big hurry to get to the Little Yellowjacket? Why get stuck out here in the snows of Colorado!"

"By jove, are we in Colorado? I thought we were in New Mexico."

"You hit Colorado when you crossed the pass."

"Well, splendid. Why am I here? Because it's an adventure. My word, you've no idea how boring life in England can be."

"And the Frenchman, why is he here?"

After interpretation, Fletcher responded, "He says he is here to find gold and get rich and spend it on beautiful American women. The French are very direct, you know."

As they pushed back out into the storm, Brannon felt a little relieved. Their story was plausible. Every goldfield he'd seen had attracted its share of naive foreigners. *Out West we are all a little naive and a little foreign.*

They did not make it to Brighton Pass. The sun fell quickly in the late December day. There was no twilight. Suddenly, it was dark. Brannon again located some shelter in a grove of trees and made a small fire out of the dead wood on the lower branches. For a while he worried about dozing off, but later, when the other two slept, he built up the fire, rested his hand on his pistol grip, laid his Winchester across his lap, and nodded off.

The Frenchman had the fire going and was roasting some of the salt pork they had brought when Stuart Brannon opened his eyes. He inspected the site and his companions without moving anything but his eyes. Then he stood and stretched. "We must hurry. We have to find the others quickly, or it will be too late for them . . . and for us."

Today was colder and the snowflakes much smaller, which improved visibility considerably. Even though covered with fresh snow, they found the trail that led down from the pass.

"They have been by here, and we have missed them!" Stuart Brannon pointed at tracks not completely covered yet. "Three, four, maybe five men."

"Mr. Trudeaux asks where are the children's footprints?"

"He's right. These are the men. How many did you say were left?"

"Miles and McHenry, but Miles couldn't walk, he's wounded. Then there was Tristo Lanier and the Mulroneys."

"That's five adults, but what about the children?"

"Maybe they carried them," Fletcher suggested.

"Maybe these are other men."

"Savages?"

"No, they are wearing big boots, not moccasins."

"What are you saying?"

"All sorts of people want to get up to that goldfield. Maybe some others came through the pass."

"Then they would have helped the others."

"Not necessarily. It depends on who or what their god is."

"I beg your pardon?" Fletcher puzzled.

"Never mind. We will have to go on uphill and inspect that area. We can't come this close and not double-check on the ones you left behind," Brannon insisted.

The others offered no argument, and the three trudged up the hill toward Brighton Pass. They would have missed the site completely if the Frenchman hadn't wandered off the main trail and tripped over a snow-covered body.

"Good heavens, man, it's Lanier! Is he dead?"

Brannon bent down in the snow and examined the body. "He's dead, all right."

"If Lanier couldn't survive the cold, how could any of them? He was a very sturdy man."

"He didn't die of the cold. There's a bullet hole through his chest." Brannon looked up at the two men, trying to catch their expression. "Are you sure the Frenchman didn't know this body was over here?"

Fletcher translated, then reported back. "He is very insulted. Do you accuse him of murder?"

"Nope. But if he just happens to wander off and stumble over three or four more bodies, I will get mighty suspicious."

"Maybe the Indians came back?" Fletcher offered.

"Why would they? Did you have something they wanted?"

"Oh, no. But you know, just to kill."

Brannon strained to look through the storm. He spoke to the men, but his eyes searched the horizon. "Indians don't kill for sport. They kill to get something, or they kill for revenge. They don't risk their lives for nothing to gain. Drag your friend over under those trees, and let's search for the others. Lanier didn't have his gun drawn, so he wasn't expecting to get shot."

Brannon and Fletcher searched through the snow, but the Frenchman stayed near the trees.

"What's the matter with Trudeaux?" Brannon shouted.

"He is afraid if he finds another body, you will shoot him."

Brannon waved his hands over his head. "Tell him I didn't mean it. Come on. Help us look for the others," he yelled.

It turned out to be Edwin Fletcher who found Miles and McHenry. They had been shot and pushed into a shallow, yet uncovered hole.

The three men stared down at the sight.

"I don't think I want to keep looking." Fletcher's normally fluent speech was broken. "I do not want to look down at the children."

The men walked away from the bodies and back into the clearing. "We have to search for them." Brannon finally spoke.

"I know. Maybe you were right. Maybe I have no business in this country," Fletcher sighed.

"No, I didn't mean that. Tell me, where did you last see the Mulroneys?"

"Mr. Trudeaux says they found a small shelter in the mountain. A cave."

"Which direction?"

"He's not sure."

"It could be they are hiding." Brannon motioned for the others to look to the east of the trail, as he searched the west. There was about a foot of new snow to wade through, then a hard crust, with anywhere from one to three more feet under the crust. Making his steps deliberate and soft, Brannon could keep from breaking through to the hip-deep snow cover.

"Mr. Mulroney!" he called. "Mrs. Mulroney! Sean! Stephen! Sarah!"

Even in the storm, his words echoed off the trees. He hiked through the thickness of the forest where the snow was shallow, searching the rocks for a cave or indentation. Carrying his rifle low, he circled a wide cedar and was startled to come face to face with a short, young lady with coal-black hair, gripping two extremely frightened children.

"God of heaven, have mercy on us!" she cried out.

"Mrs. Mulroney?" Brannon spat out the words a syllable at a time.

She nodded.

"Look, I'm with Edwin Fletcher and Henri Trudeaux. We have come back to help you."

He turned to lead them back to the clearing. She did not move. "Please, come!"

She stood motionless.

"Fletcher! Trudeaux! Over here! Hurry!" he called.

The two men ran through the snow, tripping and then picking themselves up again.

"Mrs. Mulroney? Mrs. Mulroney, it's me, Edwin Fletcher," he yelled as he approached.

Finally, the woman broke down and began to cry. She clutched Fletcher's arm as he and Trudeaux helped her and her children down the mountain into the clearing.

"This is Mr. Stuart Brannon. He has a warm cabin down the road. We have some food. Please tell us, where is your husband?"

"He . . . when the shooting started, Stephen ran into the trees. Peter, that's my husband, ran after him, but I have not seen them since."

"When did the shooting start? Who are the five men who came through?"

"I don't know. We were up here in the shelter. It was about dark, last night. Mr. McHenry was digging a grave for Mr. Miles, who, poor soul, died from his wounds from the Indian fight. These five men came down from the pass. They were on foot and came down between that cliff and the trees. Then Mr. McHenry shouted to Mr. Lanier. There were several shots, and both men went down."

"He called out to Lanier?" Brannon quizzed.

"Yes. But it was strange. He called him Harlan." She searched the treeline as she talked, never looking at Stuart Brannon.

"Harlan? I thought his name was Tristo."

"Oh, it is. That's why it was strange. He shouted, 'Harlan Lanier!'"

Brannon pulled some dried venison out of his supplies and offered it to Mrs. Mulroney and the children.

"What happened after that?"

Waiting a moment to chew on the meat, Mrs. Mulroney bent down and hugged the two small children. "I don't know. Peter told us to hide in the cave. We've been there since then. Are the men dead?"

"Yes."

"And my Peter and Stephen? Are they . . . dead too?" Her voice trembled.

"We haven't found them," Mr. Fletcher replied. "They are probably safe. Your Peter is very self-reliant."

"Yes, yes, but little Stephen, he's only five!"

"Ma'am, do you have some belongings? We brought these sleds along for the children and your goods." Brannon knew they were going to have to start back soon.

"We only have these two bags," she apologized.

"You start out through the mountains in the winter with three children and only two small bags of supplies?" Brannon shook his head in disbelief.

Mrs. Mulroney replied softly, "We had to leave everything at the pass. We are simple people; we do not need many things. Peter is a very stubborn man, much like his father. But I love him very much."

"I'm sure he's a good man to have attracted such a faithful wife," Brannon suggested.

Mrs. Mulroney smiled with her mouth, but her eyes showed only worry and pain.

"Look, you and the kids build a little fire and help yourselves to our supplies. Fletcher, you and Trudeaux fan out and search for Peter and Stephen. I'll . . . I'll see that these men get buried. I'm afraid they'll have to share the same grave."

Stuart Brannon hurried with the chore. As he did, his mind kept replaying the scene with the men he was burying. *Why did they get shot before they even had a chance to talk? Who's Harlan? Did they know each other from somewhere else? Where are the five men headed? Do they know about the stage stop? Can we get back before they do? Elizabeth! Littlefoot! Everett Davis!*

Brannon came back to Mrs. Mulroney and the children.

"Did you give them a Christian burial?" she asked.

"Eh, well, listen, you don't happen to have a Bible in that satchel? I mean, I didn't have anything to read."

She dug through the contents several times before she handed him a worn black leather book.

"It's the book of the Psalms," she offered.

Brannon flipped through the pages.

"What is this?" he asked. "Latin?"

"Oh, yes," she said proudly.

"Do you read Latin?"

She lowered her head back down. "No. I do not know how to read."

"Does your husband read Latin?"

"Eh, no."

"Well, why in the world—?" Brannon hesitated. "Well, I'm sure the good Lord can understand it. I'll try to read a few verses."

"Thank you."

About the time Brannon finished, both of the men came back reporting no trace of Mr. Mulroney or the child.

"Ma'am, we are going to have to all head back now. It will take today and tomorrow to make it to the cabin. We must hurry or we will all die here."

A panicked, wild look came over Mrs. Mulroney. "We

can't leave without my Peter and little Stephen," she exclaimed.

"Ma'am, they will just have to follow us. We must get started," Brannon insisted.

"Mr. Brannon, we are indebted to you for risking your life to save us, but the children and I can't leave."

"Lady, you don't understand! Those kids are half-froze right now! Another night and day in that cave, and you will all be dead!" Brannon shouted.

This time, Mrs. Mulroney looked him straight in the eye. "Mr. Brannon, it is you that doesn't understand. Life without Peter and little Stephen would not be worth living. We will stay and wait. They will come."

"Fletcher, talk to her. My word, we have to get back to that cabin before those five gunmen do. We can't wait out here in this storm!"

Edwin Fletcher took off his hat and squatted down, eye level with the children. He looked at both of them as he talked to Mrs. Mulroney.

"Your Peter, he is a very brave man. I watched him when the Indians attacked last week. I was impressed."

"Yes," she said, "he is very strong and brave."

"Do you think he will find young Stephen?"

"I am sure of it."

"So am I," Fletcher added. "And I would imagine the two of them are together now, worried sick about you and Sean and Sarah."

She nodded her head slowly.

"Don't you think he would rejoice knowing we have made it back to help you?"

"I am sure he would be most grateful."

"You know, Mr. Brannon is right about heading back. I believe Peter would want you to save yourself and these two while he was busy saving himself and Stephen."

She started to relax her forehead a little. "Yes, I suppose you are right."

"Mrs. Mulroney," Fletcher continued, "do you have a colorful piece of cloth in that satchel?"

"A what?"

"Oh, a dress or a shirt that your husband would recognize?"

"Yes, I have an old yellow dress. Why?"

"Well, if you think it's a good idea, we could tear off little pieces of your dress and tie them to trees as we head back. Then when he and your son come to this clearing, they will know for sure which way you have gone."

She stood for a moment, then sighed. "Yes, it wouldn't please him to return and find us all dead. We must leave him a trail."

Mrs. Mulroney insisted on walking so she could secure the ribbons. Sean and Sarah were placed on two of the sleds, and all the supplies on the third. With Fletcher and Trudeaux helping Brannon pull sleds, they all started back to the previous night's campsite.

Brannon hiked close to Fletcher.

"Edwin, I never thought you'd get her to leave. You're quite a politician."

"That's what Mr. Disraeli keeps saying."

"Disraeli? The Prime Minister?"

"Oh, yes. He's a friend of my father's. Didn't I tell you?"

"Look, there's nothing else you'd like to tell me, is there?"

"Well, Lord Palmerston was a distant cousin, but as you can imagine, none of us claim him after the Crimean debacle," Fletcher added.

"I thought you won that one?"

"Ah, yes, but what did we win? Can you tell me that? And at what price?" Fletcher pressed.

"You Englishmen! We're freezing to death in the Rocky

Mountains, two hundred miles from anywhere, and you want to talk politics!" Brannon laughed.

"Well," Fletcher nodded toward the Frenchman, "it certainly beats sniveling over how poor the food tastes."

The snowstorm let up its intensity right before dark, and some of the clouds shifted enough to allow sight of an almost full moon. This permitted the party to keep pressing on until they reached the partial shelter of the fir trees from the previous night.

Stuart Brannon had watched for tracks of the five gunmen, but he had seen nothing since they left the clearing earlier in the day. Broken Arrow Crossing was not on the shortest route to the Little Yellowjacket, and Brannon hoped the gunmen kept going straight up to the gold diggings.

They built a large fire at camp. It would serve the double purpose of keeping everyone warm and acting as a signal to Mr. Mulroney. Mr. Trudeaux and both children promptly went to sleep.

Brannon knew the fire could also attract more than they wanted. He sat back in the shadows of the fire, hands holding his Winchester. His only consolation being that if the five gunmen were still in the area, they could not be at the cabin.

"Fletcher, why do you suppose McHenry called out the name Harlan?" Brannon quizzed.

"I spent the afternoon thinking of that. Perhaps he recognized one of the gunmen and shouted his name as a warning."

Brannon took off his hat and ran his finger through his hair. "That's exactly what I was thinking. Did you folks meet anyone named Harlan in Tres Casas?"

Neither Fletcher nor Mrs. Mulroney knew of such a man.

"Well, I think there's more to it than just random killing."

"I'll ask Trudeaux if he knows a Harlan." Fletcher reached over and shook the sleeping Frenchman.

"Let him—" Brannon let the words die. Fletcher had started a diatribe in French.

"*Ah, merci.*" Then Fletcher turned to Brannon. "Yes, he says he met a man named Harlan in Tres Casas. But he did not know him well. Henri did not like the man."

"What was his last name?" Brannon pressed hard.

Fletcher spoke to the Frenchman and turned back. "He said Routher, or Ruther, or Rutherford."

"Harlan Rutherford! One of the Rutherford brothers?" Stuart Brannon jumped to his feet and waved the gun in the air.

SIX

"Rutherford is up here in the mountains?" Stuart Brannon stalked the campfires spitting out each word.

Mr. Trudeaux spoke for several minutes to Edwin Fletcher, and then it was translated for the others.

"He said that last month, Rutherford and his brother were in Tres Casas organizing a large party of prospectors to hike in to the Little Yellowjacket. They took a substantial deposit from each one and then started to leave town when Tristo Lanier and some others got wise and hooked the marshall into arresting them."

"They were going to take off with everyone's money?" Brannon questioned.

"Apparently. Henri said the word went around town that the Rutherfords would be gunning for Lanier."

Brannon stopped his prancing. "And they just happened to meet up in the pass."

Fletcher turned to Brannon, "This Rutherford sounds like a bad fellow. But why did you get so agitated?"

"You saw what Elizabeth looked like? It was Rutherford who did that."

"Good heavens! He actually struck the woman?"

"Yeah, and left her nine months pregnant. Look, Edwin,

I've got to get back to the cabin as fast as I can. If Rutherford ends up there, who knows what will happen to Elizabeth, the baby, and Everett Davis."

"Who?"

"Davis, the old man in the bunk who was shot," Brannon replied.

Fletcher gulped, "We didn't see any man."

"What did you see?"

"The barrel end of a buffalo gun."

Brannon rummaged through the supplies for a couple of items. "Look, what I'm saying is that I've got to take off right now."

"At night?"

"No choice," Brannon said.

"Then I'll wake Mrs. Mulroney and the children."

"No . . . I'm going alone. You and Trudeaux will have to lead them in tomorrow."

Fletcher stood to his feet. "How will I know the way?"

"You found it once. You can do it again. Just follow my tracks. If it starts snowing heavy, I'll mark the trees."

"How long will it take us to get there?"

Brannon buttoned down his jacket. "You'll be there before dark. Listen, keep an eye out for those five gunmen. They're a bad bunch. One other thing, when you get to the cabin, study it first before you rush in. There could be some trouble."

"Brannon, old boy, do be careful."

"You can count on that. See you tomorrow night."

The storm clouds were still scattered as Stuart Brannon tramped out into the night. The moon combined with the snow to provide a mystical glow among the trees. *If Rutherford heads for the cabin, and if they camp for the night, and if I can walk all night long, maybe I can get there before they do.* The whole plan had too many "ifs."

He hurried as fast as he could without breaking through

the crust. Even so, the crunch of his boots echoed in the trees. People told tales of how the Indians moved swiftly and silently across the snow. Brannon never believed the stories. *There's no quiet way to hurry through new snow.*

As he pushed his already tired body, Brannon kept thinking about the man he had never met—Harlan Rutherford.

Somehow the West attracts the best and the worst of society. An Everett Davis would give you his last dollar without a moment's hesitation. Guys like Rutherford will kill you for your last dollar without hesitation.

Sometimes Brannon felt it must be his lot in life to run up against all the Harlan Rutherfords west of the Mississippi. He was only nineteen when he refused to walk away from Big Earl Timbers in Abilene, Kansas. Then there was Lefty Ratton down on the Brazos, and Reuben Martinez in El Paso, and Chuck Stacey in Las Cruces, and, of course, a few like the one who shot Everett Davis . . . who never last long enough for you to know their names.

Brannon always had the hope that each one would be his last. *With any luck, Rutherford will claw his way up to the Little Yellowjacket and forget all about Elizabeth.* The idea didn't sound too realistic, but Stuart Brannon felt it was about time he had a decent break.

Shoving on through the snow kept his body temperature high, and the cold was not nearly as irritating. The problem was that his clothing was beginning to get wetter and wetter. There was no time to stop and build a fire. No time to search the misty horizon for man or animal. No time to rest his aching muscles or take a few deep breaths.

Halfway through the night it cleared off completely, and the temperature dropped even lower. Survival won the battle over expediency. Brannon stopped to build a fire. He knelt low into the fire, trying to warm and dry every member of his body. His throat and lungs were still aching from the frigid air, and his feet were almost numb.

If Rutherford did anything to those back at the cabin, I will have to hunt him down. Law, decency, the will of God, and future generations demand that this country be safe for women, children, and families.

Stuart Brannon mustered up his strength and kicked the fire dead. Then he plowed on through the cold, clear night. The snow reflected the moonlight, allowing him even clearer vision of the trail ahead. Carrying his Winchester in his left hand and his knife in his right, he bladed trail signals for the others to follow.

He intended to make it back to the cabin by daybreak, but the dark sky grayed, then blued before he crossed the last ridge. Brannon sat for a minute in the trees looking down on the cabin, barn, and frozen creek. A thin spiral of smoke floated out of the chimney. There was no noise or movement from the cabin. The cold winter sun was already starting to glare off the fresh snow, and he pulled his hat down to study the area.

Even from this distance, Brannon could see tracks leading to and from the cabin. *Someone has been to the cabin and left! Or maybe some are still inside waiting.*

The only blind side of the cabin was to come straight down the creek bed. During most of the year, this would be impossible, but with everything frozen, it was a clear path. Brannon circled around above the cabin and crossed the creek bed about a mile north of the cabin. Then he edged over the ice, cautiously moving among the leafless branches of the snow-covered brush along the stream.

He was in a hurry, but he knew he could not take a single chance with anyone as ruthless as the Rutherford brothers. As he reached the back of the barn, he still couldn't hear any signs of movement from inside. He took one step, then paused to listen, then took one more. Pausing next to the cabin, he removed his hat and leaned his ear closer to the chinks of the log cabin wall.

They are either in there sleeping, or . . .

He refused to speculate. Circling the cabin, he drew his pistol with his left hand and clutched the rifle in his right. His steps across the old wooden front porch were slow, deliberate, noiseless. At the door he listened once more. Finally, he kicked the door open and jumped into the cabin waving both guns and searching quickly around the place. At first, he saw nothing at all.

As his eyes became adjusted to the darkness, he spotted Everett Davis still lying on his bunk. Elizabeth and the baby were gone.

If he harms that girl one more time, if that baby's hurt, I'll, I'll . . .

He checked on Everett Davis and found the older man still unconscious. He seemed to be breathing in a regular pattern, and the wound on his back was beginning to heal, yet the incision was starting to look red and puffy.

Brannon hurried back out to the front of the cabin to take a closer look at the footprints in the snow. Several tracks led to the barn and back, and one set came in across the side of the mountain and then went back out again.

If they didn't want Everett, what did they want?

"Elizabeth!" Brannon yelled, his voice bouncing and echoing off the trees and snow. "Elizabeth!"

Slowly the barn door swung open. Brannon trained both guns on the person in the tattered buffalo coat who stepped out into the snow. The sun's reflection on the snow made the face momentarily unrecognizable.

"Mr. Brannon? Are you back so soon?"

"Elizabeth?"

"Where are the others?"

"Elizabeth! Are you safe?"

"Did you find the woman and children?"

"What are you doing in that coat?"

"It belongs to Mr. Davis. I didn't think he would mind."

"And the hat?"

"It was in the cabin. I was cold."

"Where's Littlefoot?"

"On the cradleboard on my back. I made one yesterday. It isn't very fancy, of course. What about the others?"

Brannon walked over to where she was standing. "Who came to see you?"

"See me? No one came to the cabin."

"The tracks by the cabin door, leading up that hill."

"They are mine."

"Yours?"

"Yes, I went hunting."

"Hunting?"

"If there are going to be others staying here, we will need more food. I took Mr. Davis's rifle and went hunting yesterday."

"Then those are your tracks leading away from the cabin and back here again."

"Yes, that is what I said. Why are you so upset? Where are the others?"

"They're coming in later. What were you doing in the barn?"

"Trying to find something to drag the deer back to the cabin on."

"What deer?"

"The one I just shot, over on that ridge. Do you not listen to me?"

"Wait a minute. Everything's fine? You didn't have any visitors and haven't seen anyone since we left?"

"Who would I see out here? Is everyone safe? How about the woman and children? Why did you go off and leave them?"

"It's a long story."

"You can tell me while we go drag in the deer."

Elizabeth scooted out into the snow. The old buffalo coat

dragged behind her like a train, and Littlefoot's head popped out of the back of the coat, staring in the opposite direction his mother walked.

"Elizabeth, Rutherford is still up here in these mountains. He and his men killed several of the people in the party."

"Did you see him?"

"No, the fighting happened before we got back to them. The woman and her children are safe, well, two of them are safe."

"Two?"

"I guess one of the the kids ran into the woods when the shooting started, and the father is searching for him. They might both be lost. The lady and two of the children are coming in with Fletcher and the Frenchman."

"Why didn't you have them come with you?"

"I was worried about you and Everett being here when the Rutherford gang barged in. So I hiked through the night."

"You hiked through the night because you worried about me and Littlefoot?"

"And old Davis in there."

Elizabeth put her head down and pushed on through the snow.

Brannon caught up with her. Even with the bruises still showing on her face, he could see tears flowing down her cheeks.

"Elizabeth! What's wrong? Are you hurt?"

She stopped and stood silent for a moment. She did not look at Brannon but looked down and away, which caused Littlefoot's bright eyes to stare right at him.

"Mr. Brannon, you don't know what my life has been like. When I was only eight years old, my parents were slaughtered as I watched, and my brother and I were carried off by another tribe. There I was treated like a slave. I had to carry the water and build the fires and search for wood. I was not allowed to eat with the others, but had to wait for scraps. They would not let me have a new dress. My clothes got so worn that one summer I was forced to go naked.

"The girls of that tribe would pinch me and hit me and tell me how ugly I was. That was when my brother, who was also treated badly, ran away. I thought he would come back to rescue me, but I have not seen him since."

Brannon continued to stand in the snow and study the distant trees as Elizabeth continued her story.

"When I was about twelve, just becoming a woman, I was given to a very old chief of another tribe. I was his new wife, but his old wife was jealous. She would not let me stay in the tent when the chief was there. She often beat me with sticks and chased me off into the forest where I spent the night. But if I tried to run away, they would track me down and whip me.

"When the chief died, his old wife convinced the others to sell me to Mr. Rutherford for a pony and a broken rifle with no bullets.

"I have told you already of how I was treated by the white men. Before I found your cabin, when I was lost in the snow, I truly wanted to die. The only thing that kept me alive was my baby. I wanted a chance to raise a boy that would be a brave warrior and know how to treat others well.

"I heard your voice just now as you came out of the cabin and yelled for me. I saw your eyes as you asked about Littlefoot. No man has ever hiked through the snow because he was worried about my safety. No man has ever called out to me with fear for my health. Mr. Brannon, it feels very good to have someone care about me. I think I am glad I did not die in the snow."

Elizabeth pushed on ahead, retracing her steps to where the deer lay dead.

By the time the sun was high, Brannon had the deer skinned and gutted and the meat hauled back to the cabin.

There was no sign of Edwin Fletcher and the others, but he did not expect them until dark. For the first time since coming to Broken Arrow Crossing, Stuart Brannon mounted Sage and rode him around inside the barn.

It's a long time until spring, old boy. You're going to get spoiled in here.

Brannon searched the mountainside for glimpses of friends or enemies, but he could see nothing. Heavy, gray clouds had begun to fill the sky as a new storm started stacking up against the mountains. He entered the cabin, leaned his rifle against the wall, and pulled his hat off.

"Mr. Davis is very hot. I am much worried," Elizabeth said softly. "The old chief, he also was very hot. Then he died."

"I think he's getting infected." Brannon slowly ripped the bandages from Everett Davis's back. "Let's cut him open again."

Elizabeth stepped back. "What?"

"This stuff has to drain. You know I didn't want to do this in the first place. I don't know how I ever get into things like this."

The two worked quickly, scouring the cabin for a fairly clean rag to use as a bandage. Then Brannon heated a knife blade once more. After finishing the job, he turned to Elizabeth.

"He has to have something to eat. He'll die of starvation if nothing else. Let's try sitting him up and forcing down some broth."

"What about his wound?"

"We'll just have to risk it."

By working together and with great effort, they were able to feed him half a cup of stew juice. Brannon then laid him down on his side, placing a cold wet rag on his forehead.

Brannon wanted to build a large signal fire of smoky green wood so that Fletcher and the others would not miss the cabin, but he feared that it might draw the five gunmen as well. He spent the rest of the afternoon rearranging the barn. He moved all the harnesses, saddles, and gear over into a stable next to Sage. Then he brought down fresh straw from the loft to pad all the stalls of the far side of the barn. Finally, he hooked the rope and pulley on the wheelless wagon and lifted up one side, removing the barrels that had propped it up. The wagon rested on its side, acting as a wall in the middle of the barn.

"What are you doing?"

Elizabeth stood at the door.

"Getting ready for company. If we're going to have more boarders, we will need more room."

"Littlefoot and I will move—"

"You and that baby are going to stay right—" Brannon suddenly heard the tone of his command. "Listen, I want you and the baby to stay where you are in the cabin. Would you be willing to do that?"

"Are you asking if I would like to stay in the cabin?"

"Yes, that is my request."

"Then we will stay. Are you sure the others will like that?"

"They will have no choice," he replied. "The Mulroneys can camp out over here on this side of the barn. This wall is up against the back of the fireplace, and a lot of heat soaks through. Fletcher and Trudeaux can have this spot over here next to Sage. It's the best we can do."

"Mr. Brannon, look!" Elizabeth pointed out the open barn door at the southern horizon. "Here they come!"

Edwin Fletcher and Pierre Trudeaux each carried a child in their arms, and Mrs. Mulroney dragged a sack of belongings through the snow.

"Is everything safe?" Fletcher yelled, as Brannon hurried through the snow to help.

"Yes, no sign of the others. Let me carry him." He took young Sean in his arms and headed to the cabin.

"Have you seen my Peter or Stephen yet?" Mrs. Mulroney asked. "I had hoped that they'd find the cabin before us."

"Well, not yet, ma'am. Come on in by the fire. Elizabeth has some fresh venison cooked." Brannon led the way back to the cabin.

It was over an hour later before the buzz of conversation and dinner slowed down. Sean and Sarah lay stretched on Elizabeth's bed, and the others crowded around the small table. Elizabeth, with Littlefoot on her back, stood by the fire.

"My Peter might miss the cabin at night. Could we build a signal fire?" Mrs. Mulroney asked.

"I'm afraid we can't do that. No telling who we would lead in here," Brannon cautioned.

"Tomorrow I will go out and look for him myself." She added, "May I leave the children with you men?"

"Perhaps we will all look for your husband and child," Brannon said. "It depends on how fierce this new storm might be."

Fletcher stood to his feet. "Well, I'm about ready to call this a day. I feel like I've chased Napoleon across the Sahara."

"What?" Mrs. Mulroney questioned.

"Oh, never mind." Then turning to Brannon, he asked, "How do you want us to barrack out?"

"Well, I've got you and Trudeaux fixed up in the barn along with—"

"The children and I can take this bed for the night." Mrs. Mulroney pointed to Elizabeth's bed. "It will do until my Peter and little Stephen get here."

"Sorry, ma'am, but that's Elizabeth and Littlefoot's quarters. I have a place fixed up for you in the barn."

"The barn? My children in the barn while this—"

"Mrs. Mulroney, I think you're a bit tired. Yesterday, you and the kids were going to set in the snow until you froze to death. Now you have a good meal and a warm place to spend the night. This cabin is very small. The barn is much larger and better built."

"But the children!" she protested.

"Littlefoot and I will go to the barn," Elizabeth entered in. "I heard the story you read to Mr. Davis. If the barn was good enough for the one called Baby Jesus, it is good enough for me and Littlefoot."

"Wait," Brannon pounded on the table, "let's get something clear. This is not a hotel. No one gets to choose rooms. We are all imposing on Everett Davis's hospitality. And since he can't make the decision, I will. Fletcher and Trudeaux take one side of the barn and the Mulroneys the other. Folks, that's all we have to offer. I'm sorry it's not larger."

Brannon looked at the shocked expression on Mrs. Mulroney's face.

"Ma'am," he continued, "when your Peter comes to the cabin, it will mean there will be no place in here for him and little Stephen. It would be cramped and crowded, and many would have to sleep on the floor. Over in that other bunk is a dying man. I didn't think you would want to stay in here. Besides, in the barn there is only one horse. On the other side, there are nice little roomlike stalls, one for each of your children and a private one for you and your Peter. Think how happy he will be to find such a comfortable place."

Mrs. Mulroney listened and then nodded her head. "You are right. I must have a place to get ready for my Peter. Show us to the barn, please." She turned to Elizabeth. "Thank you for supper."

"Not bad diplomacy, for a colonial," Fletcher spoke under his breath at Brannon.

The one lantern offered only a little light in the barn, and Fletcher and Trudeaux allowed Mrs. Mulroney to take it. Brannon, Fletcher, and Trudeaux sat in the shadows on the other side of the upturned wagon.

"You two will have to watch yourselves. If you hear noise over in the cabin, pull those guns and come over with caution. If those five men who gunned down Lanier can't get through to the Little Yellowjacket, they may be headed back this way."

Fletcher translated to the Frenchman and then turned back to Brannon. "What about Mr. Mulroney?"

"If he doesn't make it in by tomorrow, he hasn't a chance out there," Brannon motioned. "I'll see you men in the morning."

The air inside the cabin was hot and heavy as Brannon collapsed on the pallet on the floor. He hung his hat and holster over a rusty nail in the wall and promptly sprawled out in a deep sleep.

It was Elizabeth's quiet, yet firm voice that brought him around.

"Mr. Brannon," she whispered, "Mr. Brannon, someone's out there! Wake up!"

Stuart Brannon staggered to his feet, grabbing for his gun and his hat and his boots, which were still on his feet. His body moved by instinct, his mind still fighting to locate where he was and why this Indian girl was poking him.

"Mr. Brannon, I heard someone outside!" she repeated.

"Stay away from the door. Get Everett's pistol and get in the corner. Keep Littlefoot with you," Brannon ordered. "I'm going to swing that door open. If Rutherford and his men are out there, they'll probably start shooting the minute the door opens."

Brannon sat on the floor next to the door. Then he swung it open with his foot and pulled back quickly inside the cabin. There were no shots, no shouts, no noise at all. The cold night air chilled him to the bone.

With his pistol drawn and carried in his right hand, he crawled out the open doorway onto the porch. He squinted, trying to spot anything moving in the night. There was no movement around the barn or out in the clearing that led from the trail to the cabin.

Suddenly, Brannon spotted something or someone straight ahead of him, lying flat in the snow.

It looked like someone sneaking up on the cabin. He pointed his gun, cocked it, and waited a moment.

"All right, mister, get your hands up in the air, nice and slow."

The man refused to move.

SEVEN

He called to the man once more, "Who are you and what do you want!"

The cold, night air hung silent around them.

Stuart Brannon pushed himself upon his knees and edged toward the fallen man. He kept scanning the shadows, expecting gunshot from another direction.

None came.

When he reached the man, he pointed the gun at the man's head and grabbed his shoulder. The man still didn't move. Finally, Brannon rolled him over.

Still no response.

When he realized the man was unconscious, he reholstered his gun, grabbed the man under both arms, and dragged him across the porch and into the cabin.

"Who is he?" Elizabeth asked.

"I have no idea, but he seems to be near frozen." Brannon pulled the man up by the fire. "Do you recognize him? Is he one of Rutherford's men?"

"Not that I know of, but he could be." She motioned with her hands as she spoke.

"Pull those blankets off the floor, and let's wrap them around him. We can't get him too close to the fire too soon, especially if he's frostbit at all."

"I'll boil some coffee," she offered. Elizabeth lit the lantern and stirred up the fire.

"Mulroney!" Brannon spun towards the blanket-wrapped man. "I'll bet this is Mulroney."

"But the other child? Where's the child?"

"We've got to get him conscious and find out. Maybe he had to leave the boy out there somewhere. Elizabeth, I'm going to slip out and see if I can wake Fletcher to come identify this fellow. I don't want to wake Mrs. Mulroney under false assumptions."

Brannon quickly returned from the barn with a groggy Fletcher in tow.

"Good heavens, man, I'm moving as quick as I can," Fletcher complained. "I was dreaming that Queen Vic had died, and Edward asked me to lead the government."

"Well, I'm not the king of England, but I do want you to do something. Is this man—"

"Mulroney! My word, it's Peter Mulroney!"

"OK, listen. Go get the missus. Then you and Trudeaux take the lantern and go around the outside of the barn and the clearing to see if the child is out there. And keep a gun drawn. You never can tell who you will run into. Elizabeth, it looks like we'll have everyone in this little room after all."

Mrs. Mulroney rushed into the cabin, barefoot and dragging a blanket she had wrapped around her. Her uncombed hair twisted to one side of her face, and the obvious strain in her eyes made her look thirty years older.

"Peter! Oh, Peter!" She embraced the bulk of a man and rocked him in her arms. "Oh God, have mercy on us, have mercy on us!" Tears streamed down her face. "He will be fine, yes, he will be fine."

Brannon stepped closer to the fireplace. "Ma'am, I think he's just exhausted from staggering through this stormy night. The best thing in the world is for you to hold him just like that. Will the children be all right in the barn, or do you want me to bring them over here?"

"Let them sleep for now . . . Stephen! Where is Stephen?" Her eyes darted frantically around the dimly lit room.

"He was not with your husband," Brannon apologized. "I've sent Fletcher and Trudeaux out to look for him, and I will go and look also. But we can't see very much in the darkness."

"He must be here. My husband would not go off and leave him!"

"Ma'am, we'll do what we can."

"Peter! Peter! Wake up! Where is Stephen?" She shook her husband, but found no response.

It was about two hours later, just before daylight, when Brannon, Fletcher, and Trudeaux sloshed back into the cabin.

"We followed his tracks as far as we could, but there was no sign of the boy." Brannon pulled off his hat and banged it against a rafter.

"How's Peter?" Fletcher added, as he drew near the roaring fire.

"He's coming around, but he hasn't made any sense yet." Mrs. Mulroney still rocked her husband. "Several times he has mumbled something about it being such a savage land or savages in the land."

"Try to get something warm down him," Brannon called. "Fletcher, as soon as you and Trudeaux thaw out, go on back to the barn and get some sleep. We might need to head out soon."

"What about you?" Elizabeth spoke. "When will you get some rest?"

"About spring. How's your other patient?" Brannon nodded towards Everett Davis.

"Oh . . . I've forgotten to check." Elizabeth turned towards the far end of the cabin after Fletcher had exited and bumped into Trudeaux, who was trying to squeeze out the door of the crowded room.

Trudeaux stepped back out of her way and with a polite wave of the hand exclaimed, *"Pardonnez-moi, madame."*

Suddenly, from behind the tarp hanging in the center of the cabin came the raspy, half-whispered, half-shouted words, *"Fermez la bouche."*

Mrs. Mulroney stopped rocking her husband's head and turned to stare.

Elizabeth froze in her tracks.

Brannon reached for his gun.

Only Trudeaux seemed at ease.

"Comment allez-vous, mes amis?"

Davis's raspy voice switched to English, "Very hungry. Are you holding a rendezvous in my cabin?"

Trudeaux turned and spoke in halting tones, "He said—"

"I heard what he said!"

Stuart Brannon hurdled one of the benches next to the table to get to Everett Davis's bed.

"Everett? Everett! Are you all right?"

The older man was still propped up against the wall where he and Elizabeth had left him. His speech was slow and deliberate, but each word echoed through the room.

"Good heavens, Brannon, of course I'm not all right. One minute you're reading the good book over my dying body, and the next I wake up with a room full of mourners. It ain't spring yet, is it?"

"No, not hardly. These folks got stranded in Brighton Pass. How's your back?"

"Did you get that bullet out?"

"With Elizabeth's help."

"What did you open me up with, an axe?"

"I told you I didn't want to do it. Not the first time or the second time."

"Two times? You had to take two tries? Remind me not

to get shot with you around. Where's some food? I haven't eaten anything since yesterday."

"It's been a lot longer than that, but take it easy," Brannon cautioned. "Can you move your arms?"

"Sure, but everything is stiff. I'm not sure my legs are working, and I'm not too sure I want to find out."

Brannon turned to help Elizabeth round up some food while Davis finished a conversation in French with Trudeaux. The Frenchman leaned over to shake hands with Davis and then started out the door.

Everett Davis rubbed his beard and wiped his forehead. "This cabin is too hot. When I first woke up, I figured I had died and gone to . . . but then I saw Elizabeth and I knew it just couldn't be. The baby! My stars, how's the baby?"

Brannon brought some water and food to the bedside. "I think the little warrior is just as handsome as his mother. Everett, I didn't know you spoke French."

"Spent the winter of '66 up in Canada with an old trapper looking for gold on the Fraser River. He wouldn't talk nothing but French."

"Trudeaux never spoke anything but French. Fletcher told us he couldn't speak English."

"Fletcher, is that the Englishman?"

"Yeah, he's over in the barn."

Everett Davis smiled, "Well, Trudeaux said he only speaks French to enjoy what a fool the Englishman makes in his pronunciation."

"How's that baby?" Davis called to Elizabeth.

"Mr. Davis, Littlefoot is going to be a very strong warrior."

"Brannon, are all these people staying with us? You've got to stop running this place like a hotel. We take in any more, and you and me will be sleeping in the snow."

"Listen, you relax and eat something. I'll fill you in on what's happened during your nap."

The two men talked quietly until way past daybreak. Then Everett Davis drifted off to sleep.

The heavy clouds turned to snow before noon, and everyone spent the day crowded into the cabin. The most anyone could get from Mr. Mulroney was an occasional reference to "savage land." After he had been spoon-fed some dinner by his wife, Mulroney slept again. For the first time in twelve hours, Mrs. Mulroney left her husband's side and gathered the children to go back out to the barn.

"The storm is pretty bad, ma'am. Let me carry the children," Brannon offered. She had Sarah in her arms already, so he scooped up Sean.

"Are you going to find my brother?" he asked.

Stuart Brannon looked at the thin little boy. "When the storm lets up a little, I will try."

"Mrs. Elizabeth says that you could find a white rabbit in the snow. Is that true?"

"Well, sure. All you got to do is look for the pink on the bottom of their toes," Brannon laughed.

"Mr. Brannon," Sean questioned, "did you ever shoot anybody?"

"What?"

"My daddy wears a gun, but he said he has never shot anybody. Did you ever shoot anybody?"

"Sean!" Mrs. Mulroney quieted the boy. Brannon let the question drop.

They shook the snow off their coats as they entered the barn. The well-built structure offered complete protection from the storm, but it was considerably colder than the small cabin. Brannon looked after Sage and glanced over to where Fletcher and Trudeaux slept. Suddenly, he had an idea. He spun toward the barn door and kicked his way back across the snow and around to the cabin.

"Everett! Hey, Everett. Are you asleep?"

"Yeah, would you bring me a piece of Nadine Montgomery's big apple pie?"

"Man, that's the fastest recovery I've ever seen. You're already dreaming about the widow Montgomery?"

"The pie, boy, I said bring me the pie."

"Everett, this cabin and the barn share a common wall, right?"

"Yep. The wall behind the big bunk over there, running right up to the fireplace."

"Is that the wall where the grain sacks are stacked in the barn?"

"I reckon so. Why?"

"Well, look, the barn door faces the corral on the south; the cabin door is way around here on the east. It's a long, cold walk between the two. What if I cut a doorway right where that bunk is, and we could save everyone a few steps. Maybe we could make the barn a bit warmer."

"And this room cooler?"

"Right."

Davis shrugged, "It's all right by me, but you're going to have your work cut out. The only bucksaw I know of is broke. You'll have to use an axe. It will take a long time."

"We've got all winter," Brannon grimaced.

About dark Mr. Mulroney came to and called for his wife. Hair neatly in place this time, she hurried to his side.

"The savages rule the land." He choked back tears.

"What?"

"The savages, the Indians! They have carried off little Stephen, and I've lost him in the snow. I swear to heaven, I just couldn't find them again."

"The savages have our little Stephen!" She looked over at Elizabeth, who carried Littlefoot on the cradleboard. Elizabeth just looked down at the floor.

"Go get Brannon," Everett Davis called out from his bunk.

Elizabeth hurried out to the barn, and soon the whole group gathered at Mulroney's side to hear the story. The tall Irishman sat up on the straw pallet and leaned against the wall as he began.

"I followed Stephen's tracks until dark that first day. They led to a grove of white-barked trees and a campfire. I could see him standing near the fire and several Indians, maybe six or seven, standing around. I decided that I would wait until dark, then sneak in, and grab him."

"I waited behind some rocks. Then, may God forgive, I fell asleep. When I awoke, it was dark, so I began to crawl toward their camp. Only when I got there, the camp was gone! They had moved out. I was panicked! I tried to pick up some tracks, but could see very little in the night. By daylight, the snow had blown the tracks clean. I've been wandering in the woods trying to find Stephen. Then I found the yellow ribbons and came here. We must go look for little Stephen."

"Dear God, have mercy on us," Mrs. Mulroney cried over and over.

"I must go out and look for Stephen." Peter Mulroney struggled to his knees.

Brannon put his hand on the Irishman's shoulder.

"Wait. Get your rest. You will need strength, and we can't go out now. It's dark, and there's a very bad snowstorm."

"Stephen needs me," Mulroney insisted.

"And so do Sean and Sarah." When the weather allows, we'll all go out.

Mrs. Mulroney wailed, "What will they do with Stephen? Will they eat him? We have heard such stories."

"What? You heard what?" Elizabeth gasped.

"On the boat, we heard that the savages . . ." Mrs. Mulroney stared at Littlefoot, who gazed around the room from his mother's back, comfortably ignorant of all that was happening. "I'm sorry," she confessed, "I'm very scared. Will they hurt him?"

Brannon stood next to Elizabeth and sighed. "Well, I can't say for sure. But if those are the same bunch I ran across, then they were just a small hunting party that got snowed in up here in the mountains between the passes. I would guess they'll hold him for barter."

"Barter?"

"They might show up wanting to trade him for a horse or some food or a rifle—whatever they need."

Mulroney collapsed back on the straw pallet. "We will look for him tomorrow."

Elizabeth and Brannon left the Mulroneys in the cabin to walk out to the barn.

"This is a very bad storm," she motioned.

"I don't think we'll be going anywhere tomorrow."

"Does Mrs. Mulroney hate me?" she asked.

Brannon opened the barn door, and they both stepped out of the blowing snow.

"No, she's just a very frightened lady. People say strange things when they are scared."

Elizabeth slipped off the blanket she used as an overcoat and took Littlefoot out of the cradleboard. "Let me tell you something, Mr. Brannon. When I was a little girl still in the land of my parents, my mother's mother would tell us all about the white men. I can still see her bending low, looking into my eyes and saying, 'Watch out for white men. They eat little ones like you!'"

"Well, there are scared people all over," Brannon shrugged. "I guess we use the same techniques."

"Are you really going out tomorrow?" she asked.

"I doubt it. If this storm keeps up like this, we are going to be lucky to find the barn door. That's why I've got to cut through the wall. This storm might hang in here for days."

Even in his most pessimistic mood, Brannon had no idea it would be sixteen days and four feet of snow before any of them would see sunlight again. They were not easy days.

Two days after Peter Mulroney found the cabin, he and his wife packed some belongings and insisted on pushing out into the storm.

"You can't go out in this!" Brannon insisted.

"You'll have to shoot me to stop me," Mulroney replied.

"Look, you are not going to last one day out there. If it weren't connected to the cabin, we couldn't even find the barn! My word, man, think of your wife! You'll kill her!"

"I am dying every day Stephen is not here," she stoically replied.

Brannon blocked their way to the barn door. "Listen, I hiked into a storm half this bad to find you and the kids. I will go out with you again at the first sign of a change in the storm. But your death is of no advantage to Stephen."

Mrs. Mulroney coldly looked up at him, "Mr. Brannon, if you had children, you would understand. We must do everything for him."

Stuart Brannon looked her in the eyes, "Ma'am, my boy died, and so did my wife. I don't know how you feel, but I certainly know the emptiness and pain of grief . . . I don't want that for either your husband or your children."

The young Irish woman looked to the floor, "Forgive me. My Peter says I speak without thinking. Maybe he is right."

"Folks, your Stephen is with the Indians. Now that's not the best of situations, but it is better than being lost in the woods. He will have food, fire, and no animal attacks. They are trapped up here like we are. They can't carry him off until spring. We will find them before then. We should gain our full strength and pray for the storm to end."

Mr. Mulroney stood at the door and stared out into a storm that cut the visibility to only a few feet. The huge, wet snowflakes stuck to everything they touched, turning the porch, cabin, and barn to icy white. Except where the path was shoveled back to the cabin, a person would have to push through waist-deep snow to advance in any direction.

Peter Mulroney turned back to his wife. "We will wait one more day."

She turned to Brannon. "Do you believe in prayer?"

He cleared his throat, "Well, sure. I mean, doesn't everyone?" Brannon walked away from the Mulroneys and went to the far wall where Fletcher and Trudeaux were trying to chop through one of the logs joining the cabin. He took the axe away from Edwin Fletcher and began throwing his strong shoulder into the work. His mind, however was in Arizona.

Sure I believe in prayer. I prayed for Lisa, and she died. I prayed for that baby, and he died. I prayed those cows would live, and they died. I believe in praying. I'm not so sure I believe in getting prayers answered.

Each day Peter Mulroney would pack up and get ready to head out into the storm, and everyday the fierceness of the gale would force him to remain. Each day ate away at his patience and reason.

At the end of the first week, Brannon, Fletcher, and Trudeaux had chipped out a hole three feet wide and one foot high. They could not crawl through yet, but they could hand supplies and food from the cabin into the barn.

Sometime near daylight one morning, Brannon, Everett Davis, and Elizabeth woke up to the voice of Mrs. Mulroney calling out through the pass hole.

"Mr. Brannon, my Peter has left. He is beside himself. I couldn't stop him."

"When did he leave?" Brannon grabbed his coat.

"Only a few minutes ago. I thought he was coming to tell you, but I didn't hear him come to the cabin."

Brannon pulled on his boots, grabbed his gun and holster

off the wall, and jammed on his hat. Then turning to Elizabeth, he called out, "I'll be back soon."

Mulroney was not difficult to track even in the horrible storm. He had plowed a deep trail in the snow, and since he was only a few minutes ahead of Brannon, the heavy snow was unable to fill it in.

Still Stuart Brannon knew that Mulroney was a driven man. He did not slow his pace, even though he was unsure of what direction to head. Brannon was having a hard time catching up. He figured Mulroney was actually heading back up the trail towards the Little Yellowjacket. Visibility was not more than five feet, but all Brannon had to do was follow Mulroney's trench.

Suddenly shots rang out up ahead. Brannon cocked his Winchester and dropped to the snow. There were six quick shots and then a piercing yell.

It was Peter Mulroney's voice.

Brannon ran, stumbled, fell, got up, and ran on through the snow. He was almost on top of them before he could see what was happening. Mulroney was down on all fours in the snow, swinging the barrel of his gun wildly at four growling gray wolves.

A quick shot from Brannon's rifle brought down the largest of the animals. Then, quickly, the others scattered and were gone.

Peter Mulroney's voice shook as he stood to his feet.

"They came on me from nowhere. I didn't hear them or see them. How did I miss them? I shot all six bullets and didn't hit a one!"

"You were caught off guard. Come on, let's go back to the Crossing," Brannon urged.

"No! This is precisely why I must find Stephen . . . before the wolves devour him."

"Mulroney! Listen. Let's talk man to man. If your Stephen is alone in these woods, he is dead . . . the snow, the wolves—

he can't survive. If he's with the Indians, they will keep him alive. A dead hostage is worth nothing to them."

"I am going on. Don't try and stop me."

"I am stopping you." Brannon leveled the Winchester rifle at Mulroney.

"Then you will shoot me in the back." Mulroney turned and headed away.

Brannon grabbed him around the neck with his free left arm and pulled him backwards. Mulroney countered with a barrage of shattering blows to Brannon's midsection with his elbows. Then he spun loose and threw his weight behind a right-hand punch that landed squarely on Brannon's nose. His rifle dropped into the snow.

Brannon jumped to his feet and threw a number of quick, powerful jabs. Then he caught Mulroney's chin with a round-house right. The Irishman stumbled backwards and went down, allowing Brannon to leap for him. A kicking foot caught Brannon in the stomach and knocked the wind out of him.

Gasping for air, Brannon fended off two more punches, jumped behind Mulroney, and locked his arm behind the man's head. Mulroney fell face first into the snow, and Brannon was on top of him. Holding the Irishman down, he struggled to get a breath.

"Mulroney, we're on the same side! My word, what are you doing?" Brannon gasped.

"I have to do something! I can't just stand around and wait!"

"Did you ever track an Indian in a snowstorm this bad?"

"No!" Mulroney shouted.

"Neither has anyone else on earth," Brannon yelled back. "Let's wait out the storm. Then I promise to go with you, and we won't come back until we have your Stephen."

Peter Mulroney took several deep breaths and relaxed his voice. "Even if it takes a month?"

"Even if it takes ten years!" Brannon insisted.

Over the next days, Mulroney would rise early, stand in the doorway of the barn, and stare at the raging storm. Then he would turn, dejected, and say, "Not today, mother. We will wait one more day."

Everett Davis gained strength each day and was able to walk short distances by using a crutch Brannon made for him. He spent most of his hours telling wild stories to Trudeaux, who had decided to begin to speak English.

Elizabeth was delighted when Brannon brought back the hide from the gray wolf. She stretched it out on a rack and cured it near the fire. She had great plans to line Littlefoot's cradleboard with it. Mrs. Mulroney helped her with the cooking chores. Sean and Sarah played with Sage and took special delight in crawling through the hole in the wall between the barn and the cabin.

Fletcher and Brannon finally managed to chop through two more timbers, and the hole was now about three feet high. They decided to quit at that point, worried that additional chopping would weaken the wall.

The men spent the time making three extra pairs of snowshoes and developed a plan for the search for Stephen.

"I think that only three of us should go out, and the rest stay at the cabin," Brannon suggested.

"But we need every person to look," Mrs. Mulroney pleaded.

"We must also protect the cabin. Somewhere in the mountains are at least five members of the Rutherford gang. And we can't be sure that the Indians won't come here while we are out looking for them. I think Trudeaux and Davis should stay here."

"Then I will go with you to look for Stephen," Mrs. Mulroney insisted.

It was Mr. Mulroney that calmed her down. "You must stay with the children. There could be shooting. We don't want our children to be orphans. I think Mr. Brannon is right. We want a warm cabin and a good meal ready for Stephen."

They debated and re-debated the plan over the next several days. On January 14, Peter Mulroney went to the barn door and pushed it open. Across the chest-deep snow, he could see the clearing, the trees on the mountain, and the distant mountain range. The storm had broken. It was clear.

Before the sun was above the treetops, Mulroney, Fletcher, and Brannon hiked out of the clearing and into the trees. A small pair of snowshoes were strapped to Stuart Brannon's back.

EIGHT

Actually, it wasn't much of a plan.

Brannon convinced the others to hike over the near mountains to the east and find the hot springs. He believed the Indians would draw water there and possibly leave some sign to follow. If that didn't work, Brannon knew they'd have to hike back up to the pass to begin the search. He kept reassuring Mulroney that the Indians wouldn't leave these mountains until spring. Yet, Stuart Brannon was not all that certain.

No matter how long it took, he had committed himself to search for the boy, which meant logistical problems of survival. They carried bedrolls and enough food for around a week, at most. Beyond that, they'd have to trust Providence.

Brannon was not surprised at the stamina of Peter Mulroney. Two weeks of snowed-in frustration gave him the strength of a bear in snowshoes. Fletcher turned out to be an excellent hiker as well. They didn't stop for lunch and made it to the hot springs about dark.

"We're going to have to camp up here tonight," Brannon announced about two hundred yards away from the springs while they were still in the tall timbers.

"What? We're almost there!" Mulroney complained.

"If others are using these hot springs, they can come anytime. We don't want them to discover us before we discover them. Besides, it's too dark to get a good look at the tracks tonight."

"Well, I'm going down," Mulroney asserted.

"Wait!" Brannon cautioned. "Even if you find tracks, you can't follow them tonight. And your tracks will lead others back up here to us. We've got to get the jump on them, not the other way around."

By breaking off some dead undergrowth of branches, they were able to build a small, hot fire. The three huddled around the flames, blankets drawn across their shoulders.

"How long do you think this clear weather will last?" Fletcher asked.

"Well, I'm not all that familiar with these mountains," Brannon responded. "Texas, New Mexico, and Arizona—that's my territory. But good weather never seems to last more than three days. It's bad weather that goes on forever."

"Sort of like luck," Mulroney suggested. "I mean, good luck doesn't last long, but you can't seem to shake it once things start going bad."

"Edwin," Brannon remarked, "you surprised me. That was a tough hike today, and you hardly got winded."

"Oh, I suppose you thought I spent my life sitting around some English garden sipping tea, correct?"

"Well, sort of."

"The last ten years I've been in the north of India trying to keep the Monguls from killing the Hindus, and the Hindus from killing the Monguls, and both of them from killing me."

Brannon turned to the Irishman, "How about you, Mulroney, where did you spend the past ten years?"

"Farming rocks and potatoes and starving to death," he sighed.

"You're a rich man, Mulroney," Brannon added, "that wife of yours is a stander."

"A what?"

"A stander. My daddy used to say there are two types of friends and two types of women. One kind will stand with you no matter what the circumstances . . . those are the standers. The other kind are runners. First sign of trouble, they will turn and run. The only problem is that you don't usually know what kind you got until you're in a deep bind."

"Well," Mulroney nodded, "you're right. My Janie, she's a stander."

"Yeah, my Lisa was that way. She moved out into that harsh desert country when no other woman dared to." Brannon took a stick and poked at the fire. "'Course, she paid a price for being a stander."

There was silence for a moment. Then Fletcher spoke. "Brannon, what do you think about taking an Indian woman, for, you know, a wife?"

"You making plans?" Brannon laughed.

"Oh, no, no. Listen, I know Elizabeth belongs to you, but—"

Brannon grabbed the blanket around Fletcher's neck and shoved it hard against his Adam's apple. "She doesn't 'belong' to me! I have not touched that girl, nor will I. And the next time you insult that lady you better be drawing your gun out of the holster, do you understand?" Suddenly Brannon recognized the innocent fear in Fletcher's eyes. "Look," he relaxed his grip and sat back down, "I'm sorry, I just didn't like the implications."

Fletcher took a deep breath and relaxed. The next several moments were awkwardly silent.

Finally, it was Fletcher who spoke.

"Look, Brannon, can we have a philosophical discussion of this matter without being personal? I assure you, I intended no offense."

Brannon smiled, rubbed his hand across his mouth, and

waved his arm. "Yeah, go ahead. I promise to contain my rage."

"Well, my question is this. Since there are so very few women out West, and since, well, the companionship of a lady is . . . you know . . . enjoyable . . . why not take up with one of the native women? At least, while you search for gold, or hunt bison, or whatever."

"It's wrong."

"You mean, wrong for a white man to mate with a savage?" Fletcher continued.

"I'm sure glad this is only philosophical." Brannon could feel the anger rise. "It's wrong to treat women like cattle or sheep, no matter what their color. If you want an Indian for a wife, you've got to find one that wants to marry you. Then you get her father's permission. Then you take her to town to a church and get a proper wedding, and then you be a stander, because she's the only wife you're going to get."

Again, a long silence.

Finally, Fletcher replied, "Then you won't be taking an Indian for a wife, I assume?"

"Not an Indian . . . not a white . . . not an Oriental. I've got a wife," Brannon insisted.

"But she died—" Mulroney broke into the conversation.

"Oh, she died, all right, but she lives in my heart. You see, it was my heart that was in love with her. It was my heart that I gave to her, and my heart hasn't changed. There won't be another woman for Stuart Brannon."

"Ah, time will tell," Fletcher nodded.

"You haven't been eyeing Elizabeth for yourself?" Brannon inquired.

"Not yet—" Fletcher began.

"Well, don't. First of all, she's too good for you. And second, she'd turn you down cold."

"Oh?"

"Elizabeth's one goal in life is to raise Littlefoot to be a brave warrior. She has no desire to get him mixed up again with white society."

"Well, I think you—" Fletcher started.

"I think we better get some rest." Brannon kicked snow on the fire and lay back down, pulling his bedroll over him.

Brannon sat up and looked out at the pale gray night sky. Even as the last morning stars faded, he could tell it would be another clear day. He pulled his bedroll up around his shoulders and grabbed his Winchester out of the scabbard. It felt like ice in his hands. He lifted it to his right shoulder and pointed the barrel in the direction of the hot springs as he scanned through the sights of the rifle. He thought he noticed movement in the brush that hid the springs.

He kept the gun poised, waiting. As daybreak approached, he could see more clearly.

Elk! A big bull elk. He lowered his rifle and watched as the large racked animal circled the hot springs with several does close by. Brannon restrained the impulse to shoot one of the animals. What they needed now was surprise.

As the big elk wandered to the right of the springs with one of the large does, Brannon again took aim with his rifle. Suddenly, from the far side of the mountain a shot rang out. The doe dropped to the snow. The other elk scattered in panic to the tree-covered mountains.

Fletcher and Mulroney stumbled out of sleep, grabbing for their guns. "Did you hear—" Fletcher started.

"Shh, quiet!" Brannon urged. He pointed with both his head and the barrel of the rifle.

Across the little valley, out of the trees, Brannon spotted two buckskin figures approaching the fallen elk.

"The savages!" Mulroney raised his rifle to fire.

"NO!" Brannon shouted a whisper and frantically waved

his hand. "Wait, we don't want to fight them . . . just yet. They have to lead us back to their camp."

"But they have Stephen."

"We don't know that for sure. Get your gear packed up. We'll follow them."

Mulroney hesitated. "We could shoot them and then follow their tracks back through the snow."

"If we arrive at their camp having killed two of their members, they will fight to the death before they'd give up the boy. But if we arrive, having caused them no harm, well, the odds are better," Brannon insisted.

"So what do we do?" Fletcher asked.

Brannon gathered up his bedroll. "Grab something to eat and get ready to move out. It will take them some time to dress out that elk. We can't move out of these trees without being seen. We'll have to wait for them to leave first."

"Look!" Fletcher pointed back down at the hot springs. A third Indian now came into view.

"He was hanging back to see if there'd be any trouble." Brannon added, "There could be another up there."

"And my Stephen!" Mulroney stalked back and forth in the snow.

"Look, sit still. Lean against the trunk of a tree and keep calm. We've got to try to get Stephen away from them before the shooting starts."

The men hunkered down next to several tall pines and silently gazed at the Indians gutting out the elk. The sun was well above the trees when they finally quartered the animal. Brannon was chilled to the bone.

When the Indians finished their work, they cleaned up in the hot springs and built a small fire.

As they began to roast some of the newly carved meat, Mulroney edged over to Brannon. "There's only three of them. Let's take them before we freeze to death."

"Wait!" Brannon silenced him.

After what seemed like the world's slowest meal, the Indians loaded the elk upon their shoulders. They waved up at the far mountain, and another brave scooted down to help them carry the meat.

"How many do they have up in those trees?" Fletcher asked.

"That's our problem. We have no idea. In fact, we don't know for sure that this is the bunch that carried off the boy."

The sun was past halfway in the sky when the three white men edged out of the trees towards the hot springs. Brannon knelt at the water's edge to take a drink. He motioned to the others. "Come on, this may be the last thing warm you feel in a week."

"We must hurry and catch up with the savages," Mulroney insisted.

Brannon sighed. "They're Indians, Ute Indians, not wild animals. Second, we don't want to catch them, we want to follow them. And third, they're loaded down with sixty to eighty pounds of meat apiece. We won't have any trouble following their trail in this deep snow." Brannon rubbed his whiskers and shoved his hat back on his head. He readjusted the supplies on his back, glanced up at the position of the sun, and pushed on across the small valley to follow the two-foot deep Indian tracks.

Mulroney stuck close to Brannon, and Fletcher shuffled along behind.

"Brannon, why don't those Indians camp right down there next to the hot springs? It would save time and effort."

"That's what I've been thinking." Brannon nodded. "Maybe they found a spot that has more shelter than the valley. A windstorm could really whip down that canyon. But maybe they're worried that the hot springs will be too attractive."

"To animals?" Fletcher asked. "Bears, wolves, and all?"

"And two-legged ones carrying guns. If they've run across that Rutherford bunch . . . well, no telling what happened."

As they entered the trees on the far side, Brannon explained the strategy. "Look, we're going to try to sneak right up on their camp and see if we can spot Stephen. If we get spotted, we're in for a tough fight. These boys won't get scared and run. Fletcher, I need you to drop back about twenty yards. They might not spot you back there, and you can come up as the reserves."

"Are you cutting me out of the action?" Fletcher argued.

"Not hardly," Brannon laughed. "If they do spot you, they'll hang back and pick you off first thing."

"Cheery thought."

"Are you sure you don't want to be home in England sitting down to high tea?"

"The thought crosses my mind from time to time. Do be careful."

Brannon continued the caution, "Remember . . . try not to start anything. We want Stephen, not a fight."

The afternoon hike through the woods was slow and easy. They had crossed the far mountain and were headed down an adjoining valley. Brannon kept lagging back. He knew that anytime they were close enough to see the Indians up ahead, the Indians could spot them as well.

From the tracks he could tell that they had reached the creek at the bottom of the mountain and headed upstream. He led the others up the hill, away from the stream. They plowed their own course parallel to the stream but back in the trees and out of sight. Their snowshoes kept their approach quiet.

Suddenly, Brannon halted. He waved the others down. Fletcher trailed by only twenty or thirty feet. At the bottom of the mountain, the frozen creek turned at a right angle up a steep canyon. Right at the bend in the creek, a deep cave had been carved out by centuries of spring and summer snow melt. During those seasons, the cave would be mostly under water, but in the winter it provided a large, dry, protected cavern.

Brannon, Fletcher, and Mulroney huddled together to watch the cave as the hunters returned. Stuart Brannon counted eight braves including the three he had faced at the hot springs on Christmas day.

"I count eight," Fletcher spoke quietly.

"Yeah, that's all I see, so far. They all look pretty young. Must be a hunting party, like I said. Mulroney, I can't see your son, can you?"

"No, but he could be back in that cave."

"That's what I was thinking. We're going to have to sit things out for a while up here. If they don't have Stephen, we don't want to stir things up," Brannon insisted.

"Look!" Mulroney started to shout, but Brannon covered his mouth and pulled him back.

A small boy walked out of the cave, dragging a brown blanket around his shoulders. He stood next to the fire.

"It's Stephen. I know it's my Stephen. God in heaven, have mercy on us," Mulroney mumbled over and over.

"What now?" Fletcher asked.

Brannon took his bag of supplies off his back and dug out some dried meat. "Wait."

"You mean do nothing?" Mulroney gasped.

Brannon turned slowly and looked at the Irishman. Then he looked back at the Indian camp. "I didn't say do nothing, I said wait. We have to make sure we know how many Indians are down there, and we have to devise a plan to rescue Stephen."

"Man, there's only eight. We can sit up here and pick them off one at a time," Mulroney suggested.

"Well, first you have to make sure we can kill every one of them. If one or two scatter, they will track us right back to the cabin for vengeance. Second, every bullet fired in that cave will bounce two or three times. There would be a good chance of one of the bullets striking Stephen. We've got to wait until he comes away from the cave."

"What would we do if we did grab him?" Fletcher questioned.

"That's the next problem. We can't outrun all of them. Besides, we don't want to lead them right back to the cabin and the others. We've got to head out the least obvious way."

Mulroney pointed to the frozen creek and the steep adjacent canyon, "That's the least obvious path, right up that creek."

"You're right, but we don't know where it leads or how steep it is. Yet, if we had a head start, we would always be on the higher side of them. That would give us an advantage in a shootout." The sun was casting long winter shadows, and the freezing air was turning bitter cold. Brannon drew in the snow. "The best plan would be to sneak him out of camp tonight so they would not miss him until dawn, although I don't have a lot of confidence we could do that."

"Are you going to wait for them to go to sleep?" Fletcher quizzed.

"It's our best chance," Brannon continued. "Mulroney and I will crawl up as close as we can after dark. Fletcher, you'll have to steal around to the top of that frozen waterfall. You can provide us some protection if shooting starts. Take my Winchester. I won't need it up close. You'll have to stash our gear up there too. We won't have time to come back here."

"How are we going to climb up that waterfall?" Mulroney pointed out, "It's iced up clear to the top."

"Let one of those bedroll blankets down over the edge. Somehow we'll have to climb it to the top."

"How will I know if you're in trouble in the dark?" Fletcher pondered.

"If you hear a shot fired, we're in trouble." Brannon slipped off the snowshoes. "In the meantime, you better get some supper. I'm not sure about our next meal."

Once again Brannon, Fletcher, and Mulroney clustered against the chill and watched the Indians roast meat around a roaring fire. Stephen Mulroney appeared from time to time and took a piece of meat offered to him by an Indian in a small black hat.

It was finally dark. The only points of reference they had were a few stars and the glow of the Indian fire.

Brannon turned to Fletcher. "If you stay up on this ridge, you can walk around to the top of the waterfall. But be careful. That wouldn't be a bad spot for them to post a guard. You could havc company."

"Yeah, now you tell me that."

"We'll have to give them a good couple of hours to settle down. So don't go to sleep."

"Sleep? Did Nelson sleep when the Armada arrived? Did Wellington sleep at Waterloo? Did—"

Brannon laughed and shoved his pack at Fletcher. "That's what I like about you English. Always perfect . . . even when you fail."

"Fail? The English fail? Where? When?"

"Oh, Yorktown, '81; New Orleans, '15; should I go on?"

"My word, you colonists have a limited view of history. Yes, by all means, do go on . . . literally." Fletcher bundled up the gear and trudged off into the night.

Without the snowshoes, Brannon and Mulroney sank deep with every step. In order to be as silent as possible, they inched forward very slowly. Communication was reduced to a shove or a poke. When they came to the edge of the frozen creek, they lay flat behind some leafless bushes that would have offered no protection in daylight.

The campfire had dimmed to a faint glow as the Indians retired back into the cave. Brannon crawled over to

Mulroney and whispered, "There's only seven in the cave . . . where's the other one?"

Mulroney shook his head.

"Can you see where Stephen is?"

"Clear in the back," Mulroney answered.

"We'll probably need guns then. Let's wait another half hour."

The men dragged themselves across the ice of the frozen creek and into the bushes on the near side. Now they were only fifteen feet from the fire and twenty feet from the mouth of the cavern. Still there was no sign of the eighth Indian.

Once again Brannon whispered, "If Stephen is in the back, I'll draw them out to the south. You slip in and grab Stephen and head north. Don't stop until you make it back to the cabin."

"What about your gear?" Mulroney blurted.

"Don't worry about me," Brannon bluffed. "I'll give you about ten minutes to get to the north side of the cave. Look out for the missing Indian. No telling where he is, though I would guess he's watching the south. Good luck."

"May God have mercy on us," Mulroney responded.

Mercy? Brannon thought, *God, if You're up there, this would be a really good time to show it. Lord, all we want is a little boy back in his father's arms.*

Brannon's hand stung with the cold as he clutched his Colt and crawled along in the snow. His chest and the top of his legs had numbed; their pain would be felt later. He crouched on his feet as he thought through each step. He would let out an Apache war whoop, shoot the first Indian out of the cave, and try to make it to the woods on the south. Once he got there, the plan faded.

Stuart Brannon cocked his gun and stood to his feet in the stillness of the night. A voice from the back of the cave stopped his breath and his pistol.

"White Boy! Fire!"

Brannon didn't move.

From inside the cave, he heard movement. He drew a bead for the cave entrance. The quarter moon, hidden partially by clouds, allowed him a mistlike vision of a form leaving the cave and headed for the fire.

That's a short . . . "White Boy?" Stephen! They sent him out to stir the fire!

Brannon didn't hesitate. He grabbed the boy, blanket and all, from behind and clamped his left hand over the lad's mouth. As he hurried away from the fire, he whispered, "Stephen, I'm a friend of your father's. We are here to rescue you. Don't scream, don't cry, don't talk until we are safe. Just hang on."

Brannon met Peter Mulroney at the north edge of the cave and shoved Stephen into his arms.

"Get to the frozen falls and Fletcher!"

"White Boy?" the voice from the cave called out once more.

Brannon trailed behind Mulroney and son in case a defensive position was needed.

"White Boy!" the voice yelled. Suddenly, all the Indians scrambled out of the cave.

The clouds shifted, and the moon lit up the area, reflecting off the snow. Brannon turned to see a raised rifle leveled at him. He rolled in the snow towards the eighth Indian, who fired wildly, then swung his rifle barrel at Brannon.

Brannon grabbed the barrel, pulled the Indian off balance, and struck him hard in the head with the butt of his pistol. The Indian collapsed. The guard's errant shot had traveled back toward the fire. The others fired wildly into the night in Brannon's direction.

So much for hiding which direction we're traveling.

He reached the waterfalls just as Mulroney and son had climbed to the top. He holstered his gun and began the ascent. While the others strapped on their snowshoes and gear, Brannon fired several shots back towards the cave.

They might be following, but they can follow slowly!

Brannon reloaded his guns, strapped on his snowshoes, slipped on his pack, and picked up his rifle. Then he hurried up the icy creek after the others.

There was no time and no way to cover tracks. The best chance was that the frozen waterfall would slow the Indians' progress enough for Brannon and the others to gain a lead.

Finally, they stopped in a clump of trees to catch their breath.

"I say, we didn't exactly fool them." Fletcher words were choppy as he fought for a breath.

Mulroney still carried Stephen. "I don't hear them. Did we lose them? They must be way behind us."

"Way behind, or very close," Brannon cautioned.

"Where do we head now?" Fletcher asked.

"Away from the cabin. We have to make sure they have lost our trail before we turn toward the cabin."

"How much of this running do we have to do?" Mulroney finally sat Stephen down. The boy clutched his father's leg.

"Until daylight, or a miracle happens." Brannon took one long, last deep breath and then plunged up the hill.

Within an hour the clouds stacked up across the sky, and visibility dimmed.

Struggling through the woods and slipping and sliding on the ice-covered creek, they pushed on to exhaustion until almost dawn. Then, right before daylight, the miracle happened. It began to snow.

NINE

Good weather all looks the same.

But each heavy snowstorm has its own unique ugliness and design. This one caught Brannon by surprise. He planned on one more clear day.

He had a small fire blazing at daylight. With his back towards the others, he sat cross-legged on top of his snowshoes, looking back down the trail in the direction he expected the Indians to come.

"Do you think they're still back there?" Fletcher asked.

"No doubt about it. Look at this storm. A few minutes ago, I could see down there to that big boulder—about two hundred yards. Now I can barely see across the clearing. The way this thing is moving in, we won't be able to see our feet." Brannon stood and walked over to Mulroney. "How's the boy?"

"God was merciful. They didn't harm him."

"My daddy rescued me!" Stephen grinned. "Did you know Indians don't have to eat vegetables?"

"Well, I knew there was some advantage to being Indian," Brannon chuckled, then looked at Peter Mulroney. "Can you two push on?"

"We will do whatever is necessary."

Brannon turned to the Englishman, "Fletcher, how about you?"

"You didn't train with the Prussian Army, did you?" he countered.

"Here's the way I see it. If we sit here, those Indians will find us. It doesn't take much of a tracker to follow a frozen creek bed, even in a blizzard. If we push out into the storm, we could get lost, frozen, or worse."

"Worse? Brannon, you're the most pessimistic Yankee I've ever met." Fletcher rubbed his hands furiously over the fire and then held them over his ears for warmth.

"If it was clear, we would take on those next two ranges of mountains, then cut back to the south, and pick up the trail into Broken Arrow Crossing. But now, with a heavy storm—"

"Well, if you're asking, I say let's put some miles between us and the Indians, no matter how bad the storm," Fletcher suggested.

"Mulroney, let's take turns carrying Stephen," Brannon offered.

"Thanks, but this time I will not let loose of him until he's in his mother's arms. Don't worry, we'll keep up."

Brannon and the others moved with caution out away from the trees and started across the clearing. Visibility was now only a few feet, and the snow was blowing horizontally, layering their clothes with ice and slush.

Brannon stopped, and Fletcher almost stumbled into him.

"Can you see anything?" Fletcher yelled.

"Is Mulroney behind you?"

Fletcher peered through the storm. Suddenly, Mulroney almost collided with them. Blanket-clad Stephen straddled his back.

Brannon took the used snowshoes they had brought for the boy and pulled out the rawhide lacing. He tied it to his belt and then had the others do the same. "We can't get separated in this storm. We have to get lost together."

As they pushed through the day, Brannon could tell the cold, confusion, and exhaustion were wearing on them.

Fletcher tugged on the cord. "Brannon, hold up! Mulroney . . . cut the rawhide! Said he and the boy would catch up with us."

"We've got to stick together." Brannon moved back through the storm. "Mulroney! Give me the boy."

"I will carry him myself."

"You will carry him to your death!"

"So be it."

"Mulroney, are all Irishmen this stubborn?" Brannon yelled.

Mulroney brushed the snow off his eyebrows and shifted the weight of Stephen whose head was tucked under the blanket. "I'm sorry for lagging behind, but I can't give up Stephen. Please don't even ask."

"Keep the cord tied on. We will stop and rest soon."

Brannon trudged slowly along, trying to spot some rocks or a cave or a clump of fir trees under which they might find shelter. With the visibility so limited, he knew he would have to literally stumble onto shelter.

Although they were still hiking uphill, Brannon could no longer see any trees at all. *If we are above timberline, there will be no protection from this storm.*

Suddenly Brannon's feet, snowshoes and all, slipped out from under him, and he started to tumble. Still holding his rifle, he grabbed for the rawhide cord that was tied to Fletcher. He heard a yell, felt the cord snap, and then he was falling through the air. Before he could react, everything went dark.

Arizona can get hot in the summer. Not just unpleasant, but harmfully hot. Some nights he and Lisa would sleep out on the front porch of their ranch house, hoping to catch a little of the evening breeze. Some nights they would soak the sheets in well water and then pull them over the top of them, just to get relief. There were days when the saddle leather burned his hands and the horses were so lethargic he couldn't catch a newborn calf.

Brannon thought he was lying on the Arizona desert floor. He could feel the sand rub his face raw, and he could feel the blazing sun on the exposed side of his face and arm. *I've got to get up! I've got to get back to the house and help Lisa. I am so . . . so . . . very tired. It's hot. It must be 110 degrees! I've got to get some water to the cattle . . . water! Where's the water?*

"Brannon! I say, drink this. You took quite a fall. Brannon, can you hear me!"

Stuart Brannon blinked his eyes open and then squinted at the light. He was lying, somewhere, on the dirt next to a fire, and Edwin Fletcher was over him with a cup of water.

"Where are we?" Brannon mumbled.

"Now, we've been assuming that you could tell us . . . that is, if you were . . ."

"Still alive?"

"Yes, actually."

With Fletcher's help, Brannon sat up and assessed the situation. Three fingers on his right hand felt broken. They were bent back at almost a right angle from his hand. As he reached to bend them back into position, a sharp pain rolled across his rib cage. With his left hand, he reached up to rub the right side of his face and felt raw skin and blood.

Fletcher looked away while Brannon snapped fingers back into place. Tears rolled down his cheeks, burning a trail through the open wound. Brannon grabbed Fletcher by the shoulder and pulled himself to his feet. A burning pain flashed through his right ankle, and he almost went back down. Gaining his footing, he hobbled toward what looked like a doorway or a cave.

"My word, you're a sight!" Fletcher groaned.

"It's better than I thought." Brannon managed half a smile. "When I woke up next to the flames and you by my side, I figured the worst had happened."

"And that's the gratitude we get for climbing down the side of that cliff in the snow and ice to rescue you?" Fletcher added. "Brannon, what is this place?"

"The cliff dwellers, the Anasazi. Have you ever heard of them?"

"I can't say that I have."

"Where's Mulroney?"

"He and Stephen are checking out the other rooms."

"Well, long before the present Indians moved into this country, another civilization dwelt here. They would climb sheer cliffs and dig out rooms and whole villages."

"In the cliffs?"

"Yep. That way they could see their enemy coming. But they disappeared centuries ago. I guess we wandered into one. How did you three get down here?" Brannon looked straight up at the raging storm on the mountain above the cliff.

"There's a funnel hole back there—for smoke or air or something. Anyway, Stephen found the hole next to some boulders, and there was a ladder, an old wooden ladder that we climbed down."

"There *was* a ladder? It's gone now?"

"Er, yeah, it busted to pieces when Mulroney came down. No one got hurt though."

Mulroney and Stephen walked back to the fire circle.

"Brannon! You're all right!" Mulroney stepped closer to the small fire.

"All right? Every bone in my body feels broken. How can I be all right?"

"Well, I mean, you're not—"

"Dead?"

"Precisely. Listen, there are eleven rooms in this place and one large pit that doesn't have a roof. Most of the rooms are small, and there is a very narrow, icy trail that seems to lead downhill. It doesn't look like anyone's been around for quite a while," Mulroney reported.

"Well, there's no way we're going to get down an icy trail today. What kind of food supplies do we have left?"

Fletcher rummaged about, "Maybe two or three more meals, at best."

"I'd like to sit this storm out in here, but we'll have to leave before we run out of food."

Mulroney sat down next to the fire. "You don't suppose the Indians know about this place, do you?"

"Not likely. If they knew it was here, they'd have camped here themselves." Brannon shook out his hair and held his aching fingers. "I had forgotten what it was like to be out of the snow. Where did you say you got the wood for the fire?"

"It's the ladder," Stephen's voice echoed. "Father, can we have a house in the mountain like this?"

"I don't believe your mother would like dirt floors, walls, and ceilings." Peter Mulroney took Stephen in his arms and set him in his lap.

Brannon struggled back out from under the overhang of the cliff to the edge of the dwelling to look across the narrow canyon. Then he shuffled back to the others.

"Well, take it easy on the food, and let's get some sleep. Fletcher, you take first watch. If you get tired, wake me up."

Brannon stretched out on his back near the fire and rested his head on his gear. Within minutes he was sound asleep.

This time there were no dreams or visions.

He was staring out the cliff dwelling entrance at the falling snow when he realized that he was awake. Brannon had no idea whether it was the same day or the next. His mind felt clear and rested, but his body ached, especially his fingers and his rib cage. Standing with care, he put a little weight on the hurting ankle and was surprised to feel only minor pain. *Everything else hurts so bad, I can't feel my foot.*

He rebuilt the extinguished fire and used up the last few scraps of the ladder. Then he walked about the cliff dwellings exploring each of the small rooms. There was no sign of food or wood, the two items they needed most. He went out to check the trail down the canyon wall.

They carved this trail by hand!

Brannon marveled at the foot-wide path that zigzagged down the several-hundred-foot drop of the canyon wall.

He heard someone stirring. Fletcher was walking over. "What day is this?"

Brannon smiled, "Day? I'm not even sure of the month."

"Why, it's January. Or maybe February." Fletcher scratched his head.

"Well, we will have to leave our shelter at daybreak tomorrow, whatever day it is."

"How's that?"

"We need as much daylight as possible to do some hunting."

"Hunting for the cabin?"

"Or dinner. Edwin, we're out of food."

They spent most of the day resting and searching for firewood. All the rooms had been picked clean, but Brannon found a few broken timbers at the bottom of a pit.

Stuart Brannon was trying to figure out if the canyon in front of the cliff dwelling ran north and south or east and west when Fletcher interrupted his thoughts.

"Brannon, do you believe in Providence?"

"What do you mean?"

"Well, normally, I believe in luck. You know, there seem to be some breaks in life a person gets that don't have any correlation to his status, money, ability, or worth. But finding this place right in the middle of a snowstorm . . . sort of has the touch of the Almighty in it. What do you think?"

"Normally, I'd say a man makes his own breaks in life. But this . . . well, it could be providential. But I don't understand it. I don't understand why we found it, and the Indians didn't. I don't know how God dishes out His providence, or why."

"Well, maybe some things we will never know," Fletcher shrugged.

"I don't buy that." Brannon wanted out of the conversation, but he knew his words just propelled it.

"How's that?" Fletcher demanded.

"If we can never know anything, well, it's just like being pieces on a chessboard, not knowing what's going to happen next, or where this is all leading."

"So, you don't hold much worth in trusting God?" Fletcher continued.

"I didn't say that," Brannon hesitated. "I just figure He has more important places to look after than some corner of the wilderness. Look, Fletcher, save your religious talk for Everett Davis. He'll argue the good book with you for a month just to have company."

Brannon laid back down and pulled his hat over his eyes, but he didn't sleep.

There were two subjects Stuart Brannon tried never to talk about—religion and the Civil War. Both topics stirred up pointed opinions and uncompromising zeal. But he wondered, for the first time, why he was afraid to talk about God.

There was no fire to warm them on the morning they left the cliff dwelling. They burned the last of the timbers the night before. Brannon led the way down the trail, holding his Winchester in his left hand now. The right side of his face was starting to scab over, and the wind and snow cooled what heat was left in it.

The trail had only three or four inches of snow in most places. The crunch provided good footing. Visibility at the bottom of the canyon was not as good as up in the protected cliff dwelling, but it was better than it had been two days earlier.

"We're going to cut across this wide canyon and look for a stream bed." Brannon motioned with his hands as he spoke to the others. "Then we'll go downstream until it flows into a north and south running creek. We should be able to follow that right down to the Crossing and the cabin."

Mulroney shoved his hat back onto his head and asked, "What if this canyon isn't running east and west? What if it doesn't connect with the other stream?"

"Then we'll end up in New Mexico," Brannon huffed.

He was not as confident as he had sounded and hated to have his doubts so easily exposed. The truth was, Brannon was not at all sure where they were, so he was following the old guideline of hiking downstream. The snow stopped falling around noon, but the clouds still hung heavy and low. The party rested under some trees near a bend in the frozen stream.

"Stephen said the Indians had some horses," Mulroney offered. "Do you suppose they will follow us with horses?"

"Not up that waterfall or into the cliff dwellings," Brannon replied. "Where were the horses kept? I didn't see any horses."

"Back of that washout somewhere. That's where that eighth Indian was, looking after the horses." Mulroney continued, "Stephen said that the horse Indian was from a different tribe."

"They all look the same in the dark," Brannon nodded.

The snow held off all afternoon, and they made good time. As Brannon predicted, the creek intersected another one at the end of the large canyon. The larger creek swept downhill to the left through a narrow gorge and then a high mountain valley.

Brannon rested the group about dark and built a fire. They had seen no game all day. They were all wet and hungry.

"We're going to push on tonight," Brannon announced.

"We can't do that," Fletcher protested. "We're all exhausted."

"We've got to get something to eat," Brannon insisted. "That means pushing on back to the cabin. I think we could reach it in just a few more hours."

"But it's going to be awful dark," Stephen spoke up.

"You're right, son. But if we keep on the creek bed, we can pick our way down the mountain."

Fletcher turned his back to the fire. "Until it starts snowing again."

The night was silent, like an empty room that hasn't been used in years. Brannon took slow, sure steps along the creek. No one spoke. No one coughed. No one slowed the pace. After a few hours, it became obvious to Brannon that they would not easily find the cabin.

"Fletcher, let's call a halt 'til daybreak. We should have come to the cabin by now." Brannon marched the little group over to the edge of the frozen stream. "Scout around for any wood that feels dead enough to burn. We'll try to warm up."

"I'm hungry," Stephen's high-pitched voice came out from under the blanket in muffled tones. His father set him down. Brannon took out his knife and carved off a small pile of shavings from a piece of snow-covered driftwood. Striking his flint against a rock, he caught a small spark in the shavings. He blew on it until it started to flame. Soon several branches had caught fire, and he began to feel the warmth.

Mulroney and his son hefted in an armful of sticks. Brannon pulled a green branch from Stephen and held it in the light of the fire.

"Where did you get this branch?" he shouted at the boy.

Stephen jumped back and in tears confessed, "I pulled it from the tree."

"No, no, it's OK, Stephen, I didn't mean to yell. Which tree?"

"Brannon, what's the matter?" Mulroney demanded.

"Look at the ribbon! A yellow ribbon. It's your wife's marker, right?"

"The trail from the pass? Are we on the trail from the pass?"

"Didn't you pull those ribbons off when you came in?"

"No, I left them for Stephen," Mulroney added.

"Well, he found them. We either came in below the cabin, or we hiked right by it!" Brannon exclaimed.

"Then we can follow the ribbons right back to the cabin?"

"As soon as day breaks, we'll follow the creek back uphill. We have to be close to the cabin now," Brannon sighed. He never thought a crowded, stuffy log room could sound so good.

The dark gray sky reflected dim light when they brushed out the fire and continued their ordeal. Within an hour they spotted a column of smoke among the treetops, and as they crested the hill, Fletcher shouted, "There it is! My word, Brannon, we actually found it!"

Mulroney, with Stephen on his back, started down the hill.

"Wait!" Brannon called. "Watch the place for a minute.

Let's make sure everything's all right before we barge in. The last time I did that, Lord Fletcher here and a Frenchman were waiting inside."

"Not Lord," Fletcher protested. "Just Viscount."

"Viscount Fletcher? Good heavens, you really have a title?"

"Quite."

"Look, I can see my Janie!" Mulroney called out, "I have found him!" Mulroney shouted towards the cabin, "Stephen is safe!"

Father and son awkwardly plodded through the deep snow towards the cabin. Mrs. Mulroney, hearing her husband's voice, turned to rush out to meet him. Just as she turned, a rifle shot rang out, and Mrs. Mulroney dropped face first into the snow.

Brannon whipped his Winchester up to his shoulder and with his painful right hand squeezed off several quick rounds in the general direction of where the shot was fired.

Mulroney raced towards his wife. Stephen froze in place, too scared to move. Fletcher and Brannon stumbled across the snow towards the cabin firing wildly at several gunmen who rode into view. Brannon scooped up Stephen as the two men dodged bullets.

Suddenly, a barrage of bullets and the loud cannon roar of a buffalo gun blazed out from the porch of the cabin. The gunmen on horseback retreated to the edge of the woods.

"They were waiting for us! The Indians beat us here!" Brannon yelled. He spun on the porch firing at the trees as the others dove into the cabin.

"Who's covering the barn door?" Brannon shouted at Everett Davis.

"Trudeaux."

"Fletcher, get through that crawl hole and help him out," Brannon shouted. "Everett, aren't there any gun slots in the cabin?"

"Ain't built for fightin'."

"Elizabeth, help Mulroney with his wife and keep away from the door. We'll have to leave it open if we want to fire at them."

Elizabeth, with Littlefoot on her back, was already helping Mrs. Mulroney lie down on the bed. Even in the confusion, Brannon could hear the woman and all three children sobbing.

"How bad is she?" Brannon yelled.

"She is not wounded, just very, very scared," Elizabeth reported.

Brannon fired another shot out the doorway. "Everett, slide that bench over here."

"You going out on the porch?"

"Yeah, let loose with that buffalo gun once, and I'll shove this bench out there for protection."

The gun blasted, and Brannon crawled out on the porch shoving the heavy bench in front of him. Everett Davis crawled out behind him. Several shots were being fired at the barn and cabin from deep in the woods across the clearing.

"Man, you are one ugly mess," Davis quipped.

"Oh, the face?"

"The face, the fingers, the clothes. I suppose you're expecting me to say how happy I am to have you back." Davis rested the long barrel on the top of the bench and sighted it down at the forest.

"Yeah, nice reception."

"Well, I am glad to get you back. Me and Trudeaux almost came to blows over the French takeover of Mexico, and those two ladies have been sniping at each other for a week."

"The women?" Brannon scanned the woods, but the shooting had stopped.

"Is Mrs. Mulroney looking down her nose at Elizabeth?"

"No, it's the other way around. That Indian insists that

no white woman, or man for that matter, is going to touch her little warrior. Then Mrs. Mulroney declared that no savage was going to cook her meals, so they've been cooking in shifts. Man, I never could understand how any man alive ever wanted to have more than one wife!"

"Looks like they pulled back for a pow-wow." Brannon motioned to the trees.

"Do you think they'll rush us?"

"Nope. There's only eight of them at the most, and those mounts won't travel very fast through this deep snow. I would suppose they'd circle around behind the cabin and try to blind-side us. But that will take some time. Everett, hold on to things here. I'm going to check on the others. If you see any movement, holler loud."

He crawled back into the cabin and then stood to his feet.

"How is she?" he asked Peter Mulroney.

"She can't stop crying . . . she'll be better, she'll be better." He rocked her head and shoulders in his lap. A few weeks before the role had been reversed.

Elizabeth was feeding Stephen and the other children and gave some food to Brannon. He crawled through the hole in the wall into the barn and carried food to Fletcher and Trudeaux.

"When are they going to attack?" Trudeaux's nasal accent greeted him.

"My guess would be sometime after dark."

"At night?" Fletcher gasped. "Indians don't attack at night."

"Where did you hear that?"

"I read it in a novel."

"Indians, like all the rest of us, attack whenever it's to their best advantage."

"Then why did they shoot at us from such a distance?"

"Maybe they just arrived, or maybe they wanted to know just how many they were up against. Not a bad plan, right?

Shoot from a long distance, get the others to show their strength, and then plan your attack," Brannon nodded. "Don't ever think that Indians are dumb when it comes to fighting. They spend their whole lives at it."

The afternoon was tense without any sign or sound from the Indians. The men took turns watching the woods and resting.

Elizabeth brought some warm water to Brannon.

"You are more ugly than me," she laughed.

"That's what people keep telling me." Brannon tried to hold still as she wiped his face.

"Why do you jerk back?"

"Because it hurts!" Brannon almost shouted. "Elizabeth, you might have to use a gun against Indians. Can you do that?"

"Yes. I will protect myself and the little warrior." She paused for a moment, then continued, "and my friends."

"You might have to if they attack the cabin tonight."

"I know. I do not want to be any man's slave again."

About sundown, Brannon stationed the defenses. He put Mrs. Mulroney, who had only slightly quieted down, and her three children in the barn behind the overturned wagon. He thought of handing her a pistol for self-protection, but wasn't sure she was stable enough to carry a weapon. Next he had them shove what sacks of grain they had left against the barn door to slow down anyone trying to enter. He stationed Peter Mulroney in a stall where he could guard both the door and his family.

He sent Fletcher up into the hayloft where he had a good view of the barn door and the crawl space to the cabin.

In the cabin, he placed Elizabeth and Littlefoot behind the table and gave her a pistol and Everett Davis's buffalo gun. He yanked down the tarp so she could see the door. Davis and the Frenchman sat in the shadows at the far end of the room, with a clear shot at the door and the crawl space.

"All right, general," Davis quipped, "where are you going to be?"

"On the roof."

"What?" Elizabeth protested.

"I've got to watch that blind side and the possibility of their smoking us out. It's the only way."

"If you don't get yourself shot, you'll freeze," Davis warned.

"Then keep the fire going. You, of all people, ought to know that hot air rises." Brannon slipped out the door and into the night.

He perched on the pitched roof, his feet against the rock chimney, a blanket drawn up around his shoulders.

His ears and eyes strained into the night. He didn't worry about getting cold or sleepy. He figured he wouldn't have time for either.

Within an hour his hunch proved correct.

TEN

Brannon watched the clouds blow east and the stars roll across the sky like a flower unfolding its petals. The moon slivered on the horizon, and snow reflected what light there was.

I can see them, but they can't see me, he thought as he turned his back to the high roof of the barn and surveyed the night.

Black shadows moved quickly across the clearing and into the trees surrounding the cabin. Brannon wanted to hold off revealing his position for as long as possible. He didn't want to shoot until they rushed the cabin. As he expected, they came in on foot.

Brannon could only count five, but he knew there must be more close behind. His rifle lay across his left arm, pointed to the front of the cabin. His eyes kept glancing to the rear of the cabin, tracing the brush along the creek, straining for sight of movement.

Fire shot out of gun barrels, and he heard the explosion of the rifles and the bang of lead slamming against the cabin door. Mrs. Mulroney let out a scream, but Brannon figured it was only out of fear. The thick door would hold back most any bullet.

Why would they waste shells?

Several shots were fired at the barn door and then again at the cabin. Brannon thought about drawing a bead on the next flash of light when he was startled by noise behind him. He spun around as an Indian leaped from his horse to the back of the cabin roof next to him.

His broken fingers kept him from drawing his gun quickly, and the Indian was on him with a knife before he cleared leather. For the first time Brannon felt the disadvantage of being one-handed. He slammed the butt of the rifle into the Indian's stomach. The man collapsed, but grabbed Brannon's arm on the way down. His rifle quickly slid down the snow-covered roof to the ground below.

The Indian grabbed Brannon's leg, and Brannon tumbled down the roof line, plowing the snow and catching his heel in a shake. Brannon grabbed the Indian around the neck with his right arm and hung on while the brave tried to swing the knife blade behind him. The mirrorlike finish of the blade reflected the dim light, gleaming as it sliced through the shadows. Losing his breath, the Indian flung himself towards the peak of the roof, and Brannon felt the knife slice into his leg. The men fell off the roof into the snow in front of the cabin door.

The Indian rammed his head into the right side of Brannon's face, opening up the wounds. Brannon responded with three hard left jabs at the Indian's face. As the Indian staggered back, Brannon kicked wildly at the man's arm, causing the knife to fall to the snow.

Brannon only slightly perceived the door of the cabin swinging open and someone covering them with a rifle. With his fractured fingers, he grabbed for his pistol, only to discover that it had fallen out during the tumble off the roof. The Indian dove at him, and they rolled through the snow trading punches. The Indian reached for the knife, but Brannon grabbed the extended arm and shoved it behind the man's head. Then with what strength he could muster, he swept up the knife and brought it to the Indian's throat.

"Mr. Brannon, wait!"

He rolled over in the snow without losing his grip. Elizabeth stood on the porch in the shadows, held by another Indian who leveled a rifle at her head.

"He will kill me and Littlefoot," she screamed.

Suddenly he was aware of other Indians close by. Fletcher stepped out of the barn and trained his gun at one of the Indians. Then all movement ceased.

"You hurt him, and I kill the woman and baby," the Indian blurted out, half in Ute and half in English.

"Let her go!" Brannon screamed.

"Let him go first."

"No!" The blood from his face wound was starting to cloud Brannon's vision in his right eye, and the knife wound in his leg burned like fire.

Suddenly, the Indian on the ground spoke in a language unfamiliar to Brannon.

Elizabeth shouted back, "He's Nez Perce! He says to kill him because he doesn't want to be insulted by being traded for a squaw."

She spoke to him again, then shrieked, "It's Spotted Horse! He's my brother!"

"He's what?"

"My brother! The one who escaped!"

A flood of conversation burst forth between the Indian on the ground and Elizabeth while Ute and whites looked on, neither understanding what was being said.

"What's going on? What's he saying? Elizabeth, tell these guys to let you go and back away. Then I'll let him up."

"I can't. I mean they won't back down now."

"You want me to kill your brother?"

"No! No! Please. When the flowers bloom, he is returning to the Wallowas, the home of our parents. He will take me with him."

"Well, I'm not going to lay here until the flowers bloom." Brannon called to Fletcher, "Have you got the guy with Elizabeth covered?"

"Any time you're ready," Fletcher hollered back.

"It's your move, sport." He nodded at the Indian that held Elizabeth.

"Wait, Brannon, they can't back up. You owe them something, and they can't leave until they get something. Anything less would be cowardly."

"We owe them something?"

"Yes, they say you took 'White Boy' and gave them nothing back in return."

"White Boy? Stephen? He didn't belong to them."

"My brother said they did not steal 'White Boy,' but he came into their camp. Therefore, he belongs to them. To go away empty would mean you cheated them."

Brannon tightened the grip on the knife and held it close to Elizabeth's brother's neck.

"You don't threaten my brother. He simply refuses to be traded for a squaw."

"Not even his own sister!"

"No, not even me. It's a matter of honor. I understand."

"Well, I don't understand. What do they want in trade?"

Elizabeth talked to her brother in Nez Perce. Then he relayed a reply to the Utes, who answered him back. He spoke to her again in Nez Perce.

"They say they want the big rifle."

"Everett's Sharps?"

"Yes. They want it to shoot buffalo."

"Forget it. No guns or weapons."

"They say the gun or we will both die—my brother and I."

"Sure, then they'll turn it on us. Elizabeth, offer them some food or grain or—"

"They only want the gun. They say they will stay on the other side of the hot springs for the rest of the cold season."

"Yeah, and how reliable is an Indian's word?"

"Reliable?"

"Is it true?"

"It is as true as the word of a white man," she shrugged.

"Everett," Brannon called out, "it's your gun."

Davis called back from inside the cabin, "It beats the only alternative—shooting it out until we are all dead. Give it to them."

"Fletcher, get back in the barn and lock the door. Everett, close that cabin door and keep it shut. Tell the guy that's got the gun on you to walk you over here next to us, nice and slow. That's it. Come on, a little more. Now I'm going to let your brother go as he lets you go. Then you're going to walk over and pick up the Sharps and hand it to your brother, not the one holding you. It's a present to your brother because you are our friend."

She instructed the others.

"Now have all the others except the four of us step back out there in the clearing. All six of them."

The Indians drew back into the clearing.

"Now he lets you go, and he joins the others. I will let your brother loose and go back to the porch. Then you present the gun. Tell the one holding you, I will have my gun on him. He will be the first one I shoot."

Slowly the Indian holding Elizabeth backed away, and Brannon released his grip on her brother. He stepped back to the cabin, retrieving his pistol from the snow.

Elizabeth faced her brother. As she talked to him, she took Littlefoot out of the cradleboard. While her brother held the baby, she retrieved the buffalo gun and presented it to him. He put Littlefoot back in the the cradleboard and held the rifle.

"He said before this brave warrior learns to walk, he will be in the camp of Chief Joseph."

Spotted Horse picked up his knife and walked back over to Elizabeth. Suddenly he raised the knife to his own throat. Brannon whipped his pistol out and pointed it towards the Indian. Spotted Horse smiled and then cut the leather strap of his necklace and handed it to Elizabeth. A few words were exchanged in Nez Perce. He turned, carrying his prize rifle, and went back towards the others.

Brannon straddled the porch, watching the dim shadows as they faded back across the clearing. Then he and Elizabeth reentered the cabin.

"What did he give you?"

"His bear claw necklace."

"What was all that about?"

Elizabeth set Littlefoot on the table and handed him the necklace. "It's a gift for Littlefoot. He will come back for us when the snow melts."

"What do you think, Brannon," Fletcher asked, "are they coming back?"

"Tonight?"

"Yeah."

"No. I don't think so. But Spotted Horse might not speak for all of them. So we'll keep the doors barred and a guard at each door. Plus I don't want anyone going outside alone for the next few days. Especially the children."

Mrs. Mulroney got up and put her coat on. Then she started putting coats on her children.

Brannon watched her for a moment. "Mrs. Mulroney, where are you going?"

"We're going home now, thank you."

"Home?"

"Yes, we will return to Dublin now."

"Fletcher, go call Mulroney in here. You take his guard at the barn door," Brannon ordered.

"Mrs. Mulroney, it's dark out there. You don't want to leave tonight," Brannon suggested.

"Oh, but it's so pleasant in the city during the summer," she smiled.

"Peter, take your wife into the barn and help her get some sleep," Brannon said.

"Oh, there's Mr. Mulroney!" she cried. "You know, we're engaged to be married."

Peter Mulroney held his wife tightly as she cried, "I'm so scared . . . Peter, I want to go home! I can't stay . . . I tried, you know I tried, take me home, Peter . . . take me home right now!"

Elizabeth helped the children crawl back into the barn and settled them down in the straw. Fletcher and Trudeaux took turns during the night watching the door.

Everett Davis sat at the table across from Brannon. "My word, man, you've got to quit fighting. Your face looks awful."

"Yeah, well, my leg isn't feeling too good either."

"I will look after it." Elizabeth came back into the cabin and brought some water to Brannon. "Do you have another pair of trousers? These are all bloody."

"Yeah, in my saddle bags, but I was hoping to save them 'til spring," Brannon confessed.

"Well, pretend it's spring." Elizabeth dipped a cloth in vinegar and handed it to Brannon. "Wrap this on your leg, and put on the new trousers. Bring me the old ones. I will wash and mend them."

"You don't have to—" Brannon protested.

"I know I don't have to. That's why I'm doing it."

Later in the evening with all the others asleep, Davis questioned Brannon. "It was close out there, son. If those boys had been older and meaner, they wouldn't have hesitated to kill both you and Elizabeth. You were lucky that time."

"Yeah, well, I've broken even now."

"How's that?"

"Well, I lost with Lisa, the baby, and the ranch, but won with Littlefoot, Stephen, and Spotted Horse. I guess some things do go right."

"Does that mean you've quit being mad at God?"

"What do you mean?" Brannon sat straight up and glared at Everett Davis.

"Well, you drug in here before Christmas, mad because the world and the good Lord were against you. I thought maybe things were balancing out now."

"It's still confusing. Why does Stephen make it safe, and some other boy doesn't? Why do I not get killed, and yet those three up at the pass were shot down in a minute? I like the good news, don't get me wrong, but I don't see justice in it."

"But you'll keep on doing the right thing, even so?"

"Yeah, you know I will."

"And why? If you're so doubtful about the Almighty's handling of things, why bother to keep the rules?"

"Because they're right, and anything less makes a man ashamed to make any stand at all," Brannon added.

"Well, we've had enough cold weather and excitement to last a whole winter. Tomorrow's got to be more peaceful than tonight," Davis concluded.

"Yeah, I'll take the first shift at guarding that door."

Brannon turned the lantern off and put a log on the fire.

Tomorrow's got to be easier than today. Brannon could usually tell when the worst was upon him. He couldn't imagine feeling worse. He sat on the straw with his back to the wall and stared at the cabin door.

It had all hit him when he saw Peter Mulroney hold his wife so tenderly. The closeness of a woman's love. The shared life. The companionship, the dreams of the future, the heartbreaks of the past, the successes, the failures, the embraces that would never be felt again.

It wasn't the pain in his leg. It wasn't the hurt in the fingers of his right hand. It wasn't the fiery rawness of his face. It was the pain in his heart that still consumed his quiet thoughts. A crisis seemed to be the only time Brannon could really get Lisa out of his mind.

Lord, I've waited over a year for that hurt to go away.

Brannon knew that he and Mrs. Mulroney weren't all that different. They both needed lots of rest.

For two straight weeks the sun shone. Although it stayed cold outside, everyone inside at Broken Arrow Crossing began to improve.

Everett Davis hardly limped anymore. The scar across his back healed over quickly this time.

Littlefoot bossed his mother around with smiles, cries, and outbursts of anger.

Mrs. Mulroney began to relax and would finally allow the children to be out of her sight. Yet she seemed always on the verge of collapse.

Fletcher and Trudeaux relived the Hundred Years War, blow by blow.

And Brannon began working with Sage . . . riding him out around the barn and across the clearing as the snow compacted and in spots blew clear.

A couple of days a week the men would hike off into the forest to drag back some dead trees for the fire. Brannon was able to keep them filled with deer meat, but most of the other supplies were beginning to run out.

Around the first of February, they used the last of the oil for the lanterns. A week later they ate the last of the potatoes. The flour was gone by the middle of the month, and the beans soon after. They hadn't any canned goods since right after Christmas.

Their diet turned to oat mush and meat. But there were

few complaints. The worst of the winter storms had passed, and spring would arrive soon.

However, on the first of March it snowed nineteen inches, and Brannon hadn't brought in any fresh meat for a week. They waited five days for the storm to let up. Then he organized the men to go hunting.

He sent Fletcher and Trudeaux up the west bank of the river. He and Everett Davis crossed the river with Sage and took the trail up toward the Little Yellowjacket.

The clouds blew across the sky all morning, but they didn't stack up against the mountains. The occasional sunlight kept the temperature from being bitter. The heavy, wet snow of the previous days slid off the trees in clumps. The snow was still deep, the deciduous bushes and trees were still brown and leafless. No birds sang. No flowers poked out of the snow. But Brannon felt spring.

"It's in the air, Everett. Like a bud about ready to pop," Brannon boasted.

"Did I ever tell you about the blizzard we had on the first of May?" Davis spouted.

"About a dozen times. Come on, Everett, it's changing. Isn't it?"

"Yeah, it's changing. And I'm getting anxious to get back to the goldfields. This thing up on the Little Yellowjacket, well, it might be a big one."

"Did Charley Imhoff give you a clue to where his claim was?"

"Sort of. There's a hidden box canyon on the north side of the creek. But he said no one can find it without a map."

"Did he have a map?"

"I don't know. I never saw one, but how hard can a box canyon be to find? You going to come with me, Brannon? I could use the help."

"If a better offer doesn't come along," Brannon laughed. "Look at that, Everett!"

Across the arroyo six mule deer foraged in the little greenery that was visible. Brannon steadied his arm and pointed his Winchester at the herd. "I've got the old boy on the left. You take that one on the right. Ready? Three, two, one—fire!"

Two shots rang out and two animals staggered back, then dropped. The other four deer shot back into the trees and out of sight.

They cut a couple of lodgepole saplings, tied them to the saddle, strapped the animals onto the poles, and let Sage drag the meat home.

Halfway down the mountain, they heard several shots ring out from the direction of Fletcher and Trudeaux.

"Everett, take old Sage back to the barn and dress out that meat. I'll hike up and help the others. If they made a kill, they'll need help hauling it out. It looks like we have meat for a month."

Brannon crossed the river with caution. The ice was thinning at the sides and would soon be breaking up. As he turned back uphill, he heard several more shots.

Man, those are pistol shots! They aren't hunting deer.

Brannon started running through the snow. The shots died out, and he slowed down, moving from one tree to another. He spotted a man moving quickly through the trees ahead of him. He raised his rifle. Then he recognized the figure and called out.

"Fletcher! Where's the Frenchman?"

"We split up to follow a broken herd . . . he went left. What was all the gunfire?" Fletcher held his side to catch his breath.

"Deer and elk don't shoot back. Come on!" Brannon broke into a trot.

It was almost thirty minutes later before they discovered Trudeaux. His motionless body lay sprawled back in the tall brush near the river.

"Is he dead?" Fletcher asked.

"Nearly." Brannon crouched near the body and scanned the horizon.

Fletcher kneeled next to Trudeaux. "Henri! Henri! Who did this? Was it the Indians?"

His pained response came out in French. But Brannon could understand all he needed to know—"Rutherford."

"He said there were three of them—Rutherford gang," Fletcher added.

"Henri, we're going to get you back to the cabin. You hang on. It's been a tough winter, but spring's just about here!" Brannon straddled Trudeaux and pulled his arms up over his own shoulders and lifted the injured man onto his back.

"Do you want me to follow Rutherford's track?" Fletcher offered.

"No. I'll need your help with Trudeaux. We'll have to come back for Rutherford together."

"I was hoping you would say that." Fletcher followed Brannon, scanning the mountain for signs of the Rutherfords.

Halfway down the mountain, Brannon stopped.

"I say—" Fletcher started.

"Shhh! Listen!" Brannon motioned with his hand.

"What?"

Brannon laid Henri Trudeaux on the snow. "He's dying. Do you hear that sound?"

Fletcher bent low. "His lungs are filling up."

"Come on, Henri!" Brannon insisted. "Henri!"

Both men were silent as they stared at their companion lying dead in the snow.

"What are these Rutherfords? They're crazy." Tears and rage filled Brannon's eyes.

Fletcher stood to attention and began to hum *"La Marseillaise."* Brannon gazed off into the distance towards where the shooting had taken place. He joined in the final chords.

"The day will come, Brannon, when the English and the French are on the same side in a battle, and then, my friend, no one will stop us."

"Well, if things get tough, there might be an American or two that would help out. Henri, I'm sorry we couldn't at least get you back to the cabin." Once again Brannon lifted the Frenchman to his back and headed down the hill.

"We're going to have to hunt down the Rutherfords, you know," Brannon declared.

Fletcher took a big deep breath and sighed, "Yes, I know, I know. Shall we go after them tonight?"

"No, we need to make some plans first. These boys don't sound like the type you would want to stumble onto in the forest."

Peter Mulroney ran across the clearing to meet them. After Fletcher told everyone the story, Brannon pulled Everett Davis aside. "We've got to go after these Rutherfords. Do you think Mulroney can keep things under control here by himself?"

"I think so. His wife is the main one to go off. Well, you know how she can get."

"We'll leave in the morning," Brannon decided.

That evening they buried Henri Trudeaux, and all trooped back into the cabin. Fresh meat was grilling on the fire, but no one was hungry.

"I should never have let him go off alone," Fletcher moaned.

"And I should have had us stay closer to the cabin," Brannon added. "The whole thing caught me by surprise."

To Brannon's amazement, Mrs. Mulroney did not break into hysteria at the news of Trudeaux's death. Instead, she spoke nothing at all. She just rocked back and forth on the bunk and shook a little glass bottle full of rocks. The noise soon annoyed the others.

"Mrs. Mulroney, don't make that noise," Brannon requested.

She continued to rock and shake the bottle.

"Uh, Peter, if you don't mind?" Brannon motioned to Mrs. Mulroney.

"Honey, let me see those rocks." He took the jar away. "Stephen brought her these for a present. Nice color, aye?" He handed the jar to Brannon.

Stuart Brannon lifted one of the pea-sized rocks in his fingers. He took out his pistol and, using it for a hammer, pounded one of the rocks flat. Then he tossed it to Everett Davis.

"Everett, bite into that. What do you think?"

"Gold! It's almost pure gold!"

"Stephen found these?" Brannon asked Mulroney.

"Said he picked them up at the back of that cave where the Indians are camped."

"Can't be!" Davis shouted. "There's no gold south of the Little Yellowjacket. I've checked every river and stream."

"In the winter time?" Brannon asked. "That cave would be under water most of the late spring and summer. The only way to get in there is when the river goes down or freezes over."

"Stephen, you found a gold mine," Brannon folded his arms, shook his head, and smiled.

ELEVEN

Stuart Brannon couldn't sleep.

Instead, he contemplated philosophy, history, ethics, and criminal justice in particular.

If this were back East, I'd just inform the sheriff about Trudeaux's death, point him toward the Rutherfords, and forget the matter. But this is not the East, and we'd be lucky to have a marshall in Tres Casas. But he couldn't get up here for another month, and then he probably wouldn't come up anyway. In the meantime, who knows who else is going to get killed. So . . . it's sort of last-resort justice. There just isn't any other choice.

Before the others arose, Brannon sat at the table and cleaned his Colt .45. He studied the grip, the chamber, the barrel. It fit his hand well. He wrapped his fingers around the grip and drew back the hammer with his thumb. His once-broken fingers now slipped easily into place. There is a indefinable quality about a gun. Brannon called his a "point gun." Somehow it always seemed drawn, instinctively, to the target at hand. *The best seventeen dollar investment I ever made,* he thought.

Brannon contemplated going after the Rutherfords by himself. He hated the thought of Fletcher or Davis getting shot. But he knew they would insist. If he went alone, he could ride Sage. But if they were holed up in the high mountains, he would have to walk in anyway.

Trudeaux had said that there were only three of them. Brannon had faced worse odds before. If he captured them alive, he decided to haul them down to the pass and see if they could get through to Tres Casas. Brannon couldn't imagine anyone like the Rutherfords refusing to fight. He stood up and clomped across the cabin to his gear and dug through it to find his hunting knife. He shoved it, scabbard and all, into his boot.

In the bottom of his gear bag was a brass-framed picture. He hadn't taken it out of his bag once since arriving at Broken Arrow Crossing. He reached in to turn it over to look at the picture and then drew his hand back. *Later . . . after Rutherford's taken care of—when I can handle it better.*

As the morning sky lightened, Brannon walked out to the barn to look after his horse. Rather than scoot through the crawl hole and awaken someone, he stepped out the cabin door. Standing on the porch, he surveyed the clearing just ahead of him. The snow had melted off the trees. They stood out in a dark, deep green barrier between the blue sky and the white, snow-covered earth. The long icicles draped over the cabin eaves had disappeared. He heard the snow melt dripping into puddles. Muddy ruts now lined the once-frozen paths to the barn.

Time to move on. He could feel it inside. Survival, as a way of life, depressed Stuart Brannon. He wanted to be on horseback, riding across some desert trail with the cactus in bloom and little calves kicking up their heels. Some locations are beautiful, but foreign. Some instantly feel like home. And some, like Broken Arrow Crossing, are neither.

He pulled down some hay for Sage and gazed around at the barn loft, still one-third full. *It's the only thing we've got plenty of.* He brushed the horse down and then led him out of the barn to the hitching post. He had just cinched down the saddle when he heard the cabin door. Elizabeth stood barefoot on the porch. Littlefoot, wrapped in wolf hide, perched on her back. "Are you leaving now?" she asked.

Brannon led the horse over to the cabin. "Well, I've been thinking about it."

"Will you come back?" Her long black braids hung down the front of her dress. She had her arms crossed.

"What do you mean, come back? I thought maybe Sage and I would scout around for a trail before the others stir. It could save some time later on."

"I thought perhaps you wanted to ride away from here for good." She looked down at the melting snow, then back up at Brannon.

"Why do you say that?"

"You didn't sleep last night."

"I had a lot to think about."

Elizabeth flipped her braids behind her head, and Littlefoot immediately grabbed both of them. Then she spoke, "I didn't sleep either."

"Now why was that?"

"I kept thinking of the camp of my fathers. I can still remember the tall blue mountains and the most beautiful lake in the world. There were happy times. I want my brave warrior to have happy times."

"So why did you think I might leave?"

"Because I kept thinking that if I had a horse and a gun, I would take Littlefoot and go back on my own. I am tired of this place."

"And you think I feel the same way?"

"I have seen that look before." Elizabeth turned away from Brannon. "She was a beautiful lady."

"Who?"

"Your Mrs. Lisa. I looked at the picture in your bag. Did you have many happy days with her?"

"Not nearly enough." Brannon tried to smile. "Not nearly enough."

"So I thought you would want to return to your happy place. Forgive me for stealing a look."

Brannon shook his head. "It's all right. I haven't looked at that picture since Christmas day—the day you arrived."

"Does it hurt your heart to look at it?"

"Yeah, that's a good way to say it."

"I am glad I looked at it. I had to know what kind of a woman it took to have a man who does good things. Brannon, why didn't the old chief trade me to someone like you, instead of Rutherford?"

"I don't know, Elizabeth. Maybe because you needed that brave little warrior there."

Elizabeth looked up and smiled. "Yes, you are right. I needed Littlefoot."

Brannon started to toss his left foot in the stirrup when he noticed something shining in the snow. "Somebody's spur broke, but I don't remember anyone with Mexican rowels." Brannon swooped down to grab the rowel. At the same time, an explosion crashed from the trees across the clearing. A bullet, just missing his head, ripped into the cabin wall.

Elizabeth jumped back through the cabin door. Brannon grabbed for Sage, but only managed to pull his Winchester out of the scabbard before the horse bolted down the trail towards the pass. He took several steps after the horse, then dove, rolled in the snow, and came up firing a couple shots back at the woods. Then he ducked inside the barn.

Peter Mulroney and Edwin Fletcher, both groggy from sleep but carrying rifles, met him at the door.

"The savages? They came back?" Fletcher managed to ask.

"I don't know. I didn't see anything."

"Mr. Brannon! Mr. Brannon!"

Elizabeth called to him from the crawl hole to the cabin. "That spur? Rutherford wears spurs like that."

"Are you sure?"

She pushed up the left sleeve on her buckskin dress revealing a scar along her arm. "Yes, Mr. Brannon, I am very sure."

"That means he was creeping outside the cabin during the night. Why didn't he start something then?" Brannon asked no one in particular. "You two hole up at the barn door. We'll take the cabin."

Brannon crawled into the cabin and opened the door a crack so he could watch the clearing. Two shots hit the door almost at the same time. Then the shooting stopped.

"Hey! In the cabin! Can you hear me?" a voice pierced the silent air.

Brannon pushed open the door a few more inches and yelled back, "We hear you!"

"I've got twelve men out here, and all we want is a map to Imhoff's gold strike on the Little Yellowjacket."

"You're lucky to have three men, Rutherford. There's only one thing you'll get from us!" Brannon stuck his rifle out the door and fired three quick shots at the sound of the voice.

Suddenly a barrage of bullets slammed against the cabin and barn. One whizzed through the open doorway, ricocheted off the stone fireplace, and lodged just above the crawl hole to the barn. Mrs. Mulroney began to cry hysterically.

"Elizabeth!" Brannon turned to see that she had already entered the barn to help quiet the children.

"Do you think there's only three?" Davis wondered out loud for all of them.

"That's what Trudeaux said, but the other two could have been out of sight. No more than five at the most."

"Why did they start firing from way over there?"

"So they wouldn't get hurt. They figure with women and

kids, we'll scare out and give them what they want, I suppose. Everett, how come they think you have a map? Why does everyone think there's a map?"

"'Cause Charley Imhoff went around Tres Casas flashing one and talking about a big claim," Davis offered.

Brannon yelled back out through the door, "We don't have any map, Rutherford!"

"Then send out my wife!"

The words chilled Brannon to the bone. He glanced at the crawl hole. Elizabeth climbed back into the cabin. "You men kidnapped my wife. Send her out!"

"There are no Mrs. Rutherfords in here!" Brannon yelled and fired twice more towards the trees.

Again, a dozen shots pelted the barn and cabin. A bullet flew through the barn door, glanced off the upright wagon, and crashed into the lantern. Glass scattered everywhere. Mrs. Mulroney screamed hysterically.

"That squaw is my wife. You ask her!" the voice shouted back. "Now you send her out with the baby. I heard a baby in there last night!"

Brannon called back, "What's the baby's name?"

The only answer he got was another bullet in the door.

Mrs. Mulroney, tears streaming down her cheeks, appeared at the crawl hole.

"Mr. Brannon," she screamed, "send the savage woman out there. For God's sake, send her out."

Brannon looked straight into Elizabeth's frightened eyes. "It is exactly for God's sake that I won't send her out." Then he turned to Davis. "Everett, see if Mulroney can quiet the missus down."

"Send out the squaw!" Rutherford yelled. "She's my wife."

"There's no lady in here that ever stood before a minister and agreed to marry you," Brannon yelled.

"Of course she's my wife. That's my kid!" Rutherford screamed.

"She says she didn't agree to that either." Brannon fired more shots toward the trees.

Another round of shots flew at the buildings. This time a .45 slug lodged in the wood only inches away from Brannon's head.

Brannon turned to Elizabeth. "Get Everett back up here. I'm going to get outside so we can keep this door closed."

Davis scurried back into the cabin.

"Everett, I need you and Fletcher to blast away from the barn door. I've got to get out by those trees at the end of the cabin. This place is almost indefensible. How many rifle bullets have we got left?"

"Whatever's on the table. Mulroney has his own, but he's tied up with the missus."

"Well, tell him to help you stir them up for a minute. With three guns blazing, I should make it out there with little trouble."

Brannon scooped up the bullets from the table and shoved them into his pocket. Poised to dive out the door, he yelled instructions, "Elizabeth, shut this door behind me. Then go help Mrs. Mulroney. Everett? Are you ready in there?"

"Go!" Davis yelled and all three men begin to fire.

Brannon kicked open the door and rolled to the porch and across the snow. He rose to his feet, took several steps, and then dove behind the trees. Shots rang all around him, but none came very close.

The firing stopped for a minute. Then Brannon heard shrieks behind him. Mrs. Mulroney ran screaming from the cabin door straight out into the clearing towards Rutherford and his men. She stumbled, fell, picked herself up, and kept running.

Brannon started to run after her, but three shots into the snow ahead of him forced him back behind the trees.

"I'll give you the gold! I'll give you the gold!" she shouted waving the jar full of stones that Stephen had brought to her.

Peter Mulroney dashed out the barn door toward his wife and was struck down by a bullet within ten steps.

"Stop it! Stop it! Here's your gold!" she yelled again.

Brannon and Everett Davis kept firing at the trees while Fletcher ran out and pulled Peter Mulroney back into the barn.

Both men stopped firing at the same time, afraid of hitting Mrs. Mulroney, who was now almost across the clearing. Somehow she managed to make it without getting shot. But Brannon watched in horror as one of Rutherford's men grabbed her and pulled her back into the trees.

"Let the woman go, Rutherford!" Brannon yelled.

"Let the squaw go," he yelled back.

Brannon knew he had to act quickly.

"Hold your fire. I have to go get her!" He dove back into the cabin, not drawing any shots this time.

Elizabeth stood back by the fireplace holding Littlefoot in her arms.

"No, I'm not going to turn you over to them. We've got to buy some time."

"I will go," she spoke without expression.

"No! At least, not alone. Everett? How's Mulroney?"

"He's alive . . . for a while."

"We've got to get the missus away from them fast. No telling what they'll do when they find out she doesn't know where that gold came from."

"What's the plan?"

"I'll see if I can get Rutherford out into the clearing on a fake exchange. I'll jump him. You and Fletcher charge right at those trees, guns firing. Elizabeth, you grab Mrs. Mulroney and drag her into those bushes straight to the north of the clearing. That will give them three different directions to have to cover. They can't shoot every direction at once. Can you do it, Elizabeth?"

"I can do it."

"Look, we just don't have time for a better idea. Everett, you two get ready by the barn door and spread out as you come across the clearing."

Brannon went back to the door and yelled.

"Rutherford, you bring the lady out to the middle of the clearing, and I'll bring out Elizabeth."

"No guns!" Rutherford yelled back.

"Yeah, no guns." Brannon turned to Elizabeth. "Are you ready?"

"We are both ready." She hefted Littlefoot to her back.

"Leave the baby here in the cabin," Brannon yelled.

"The little warrior goes with his mother. He is not afraid of battle." She glared at Brannon. "Rutherford will carry a sneak gun, you know."

"Yeah." Brannon pulled his hat down. "I know."

"Will you?"

"No, I will leave my gun here," he answered.

"I thought so."

"Are you ready, Rutherford!" he yelled once more.

The two men cautiously took a few steps into the clearing. Rutherford held the delirious Mrs. Mulroney around the waist and pushed her out in front of him as he came across the snow. Brannon walked alongside Elizabeth.

They moved very slowly and whispered.

"You will have to drag her out of here," he said.

"Yes, I know."

"It's a bad way to end the winter." Brannon didn't take his eyes off Rutherford.

"It has been a very tough winter," she whispered. "But I am not scared. There are two brave warriors with me."

Brannon studied Rutherford's approach. Even with a beard, he looked much younger than Brannon had envisioned. Since Rutherford had his right hand out in the air away from his body, Brannon figured the gun must be in his left hand, hidden in the folds of Mrs. Mulroney's dress. She was too hysterical even to know what was going on.

"Is Rutherford left-handed?" he whispered.

"Yes."

"I want to go home!" Mrs. Mulroney screamed.

Brannon and Elizabeth walked straight up to Rutherford and Mrs. Mulroney. The gunmen in the trees were blocked by their leader's back. On the other hand, by standing at the barn door, Fletcher and Davis could have a clear shot at both the trees and Rutherford.

"Elizabeth, do you know where this gold came from?" Rutherford snarled.

"Yes."

"Where?" he shouted.

"I will show you. Don't you want to see your son?"

It was the split second in every fight when a man knows he has the edge—a window of opportunity that only opens for a moment. Littlefoot's unfailing smile had opened the window.

Rutherford, caught off guard by the baby, relaxed his grip on Mrs. Mulroney slightly, and she flung herself out of his grasp. Brannon didn't hesitate.

He brought a thundering right fist into Rutherford's jaw that sent him staggering back into the snow. At that moment, Fletcher and Davis ran out blasting at the remaining gunmen in the trees.

Brannon thought he heard Elizabeth slap Mrs. Mulroney and then yank her off to the right. But he was too busy with Rutherford to know for sure.

Gunfire popped and exploded all around. Brannon dove at Rutherford before he had a chance to raise the gun in his left hand. Rutherford kicked Brannon's legs out from under him, and he rolled in the snow once but managed to grab the gunman's arm. He ducked a wild swing and landed another right on Rutherford's face. The men rolled over several times in the snow. The gun shook loose in the process.

Brannon could hear the shooting continue in the trees.

Rutherford kicked Brannon twice in the side and brought his hands, clenched together, slamming into the right side of his face. Brannon tried to roll away, but took another blow to the head. Rutherford let up for a moment and staggered back for the gun.

Brannon dove after him, crashing into his back. Rutherford fired wildly into the snow. Brannon's knee ground Rutherford's arm into an exposed rock. Rutherford brought his other elbow up quickly, smashing it into Brannon's face.

Brannon whipped his knife out of his boot. The cold steel pressed against Rutherford's beard before the man had a chance to raise his gun again.

"Drop it, Rutherford!"

Blood started to trickle where the blade had broken the skin. The pistol dropped into the snow.

That's the first time Brannon heard the yelling.

"Brannon! Wait! Look!"

It was Everett Davis who yelled at him from the trees.

"Look!"

Brannon didn't move the knife blade but glanced to where the barrel of Davis's rifle was pointing.

"Let him loose! Or the squaw and the baby die!"

Oak Rutherford stood on a snow-covered granite boulder holding Elizabeth by the arm, a pistol pointed at her head.

"You shoot her, and you're a dead man!" Brannon yelled, catching his breath between words.

"Then we'll all go to the grave together!" he screamed back. "So help me, I'll kill them both."

Brannon knew he should do something. He knew they were all waiting for his next great plan. It was like reliving the scene with the Indians. He grabbed for some great words that would make the gunman let her go.

But Stuart Brannon was very tired. He looked into the hatred in the eyes of Harlan Rutherford and sighed loud enough for all to hear, "May God have mercy on our souls!"

A loud boom from high up the mountain thundered down the canyon, and the gunman holding Elizabeth tumbled off the rock and into the snow.

Harlan Rutherford caught Brannon staring at the sight and bashed his fist into the already bleeding face. Rutherford then tried to jerk himself away from Brannon's grip, but in doing so, he slashed his neck deep against the fast-held knife. He was bleeding profusely as he staggered over and groped for the pistol.

Brannon started to throw the knife, but held up as Rutherford sagged to his knees. Several shots fired into the snow as he fell face down.

For a minute no one moved or said a word. Brannon rolled over on his back and tried to catch his breath. Everett Davis rushed to his side.

"Brannon, are you hit?"

"Hit? I've been stomped on, punched, kicked, and gouged. But I'm not shot, if that's what you mean. Who shot the guy on the rock?"

"My old Sharps, from the sound of it."

"It must be Spotted Horse, Elizabeth's brother."

"The other guy's dead back there in the trees."

"There were just three of them?"

"Looks like it."

"And Fletcher?"

"He took a ricochet, but I don't think it's too serious."

Brannon sat up in the snow, and then took Everett Davis's hand as he helped him to his feet. "You go help Fletcher get back to the cabin. I'll tend to the ladies."

Brannon slipped his knife back in his boot and shoved on his hat. Then he slowly walked toward the granite rock.

"Elizabeth! Mrs. Mulroney?"

Elizabeth sat on a rock, Littlefoot cradled in her arms. Both she and the baby were crying.

"Are you hurt?" Brannon hurried to her side.

"No, we are safe . . . only frightened, a little."

"Where's Mrs. Mulroney?"

"She ran into the forest when Oak Rutherford grabbed me."

"Where's your brother?"

"Spotted Horse?"

"Yes, it was a buffalo gun that shot the guy holding you." Brannon searched up the canyon, but he could see no one.

"My brother? Are you sure?"

"I'm not sure of anything, but it was a big gun, and the only one around here is the one we gave to your brother. Are you sure you're all right? I've only seen you cry once before," he added.

"These are tears of understanding."

"Of what?"

"When you were down there with Rutherford and I was here, I was very, very scared. Then you looked at the man on the ground and said, 'May God have mercy on us.' I knew at that moment I was going to die. I knew you would not back away from such an evil man as Rutherford. So I cried out in my heart, 'May Mr. Brannon's God have mercy on me and Littlefoot also.' Suddenly, I was not afraid of dying. Then the shot rang out, but I felt nothing. I was still standing there as that man fell down on the rocks dead. That's when I started to cry. It was the first moment in my life that I can remember not being afraid of what men would do to me."

Brannon turned away from Elizabeth and rubbed his eyes on the sleeve of his shirt. He looked out across the peaceful setting. A cabin, a barn, a snow-covered clearing. The sky was quiet and blue; the trees sang of the first birds of spring. *The earth heals quickly,* he thought.

"We must find Mrs. Mulroney and Spotted Horse."

"He is coming now." Elizabeth placed the quieted baby on her back. "I hear him in the canyon."

Brannon turned to search the rocks and recognized Elizabeth's brother riding a brown horse and leading another beside him.

She ran to meet him, and they stood talking in Nez Perce for quite a long while. He handed something to her, and she laughed.

Elizabeth returned to Brannon with a big smile.

"Did you invite him to stay for supper?"

"Yes, of course. He asked to put the horses in the corral."

"Certainly."

"I told him you would say that."

"Where are his friends?"

"The Utes?"

"Yes. Are they here too?"

"No, they returned to their camp. The northern pass is open now. Do you see that horse? It is for me and Littlefoot," Elizabeth beamed. "We will go to our home tomorrow."

"Tell him he is a very good shot."

Elizabeth spoke to Spotted Horse and then turned back, "He said it is a very good gun."

"Look what he brought me." She showed Brannon a handful of flowers.

"When the first flowers bloom, he said he would return."

"You two ride on down to the cabin. I'll go find Mrs. Mulroney. Here, I'll boost you onto the horse."

Brannon held out his clenched hands as a stirrup for Elizabeth to climb up on the saddleless horse.

Spotted Horse laughed as he spoke to Elizabeth.

"My brother says maybe we should take you with us. He said that I have you trained very well."

"You tell him I'm not going. You'll have *him* trained before you reach the Blue Mountains."

Brannon watched brother and sister ride off laughing toward the cabin.

It had been a long time since he had heard much laughter. Way too long.

TWELVE

Stuart Brannon stood on the granite rocks where Elizabeth had been and searched the mountainside for a sign of Mrs. Mulroney. Her dark dress would not show up in the shadows of the forest. He knew he would have to climb the mountain to find her.

Then the brush moved and swayed only thirty feet up the canyon.

"Mrs. Mulroney! Ma'am, it's all over." Brannon hurried over to the rock and into the bramble. "Let's go on back . . . Sage!"

The tall horse waited stoically for Brannon's approach.

"Well, boy, let's do some tracking."

He easily picked up the woman's trail. She was headed straight up the first mountain ridge north of the cabin. Brannon allowed Sage to progress at a moderately slow, steady pace. The saddle felt good. He stood in the stirrups and stretched out his legs, then settled back down. He reached over and patted Sage on the neck.

"It's been a long winter, old boy. What do you say we find a better climate next year?"

Some men learn to ride a horse at an early age. Some men never seem to really learn. And there are a few, like Brannon, who were born to ride. He never quite felt at ease until he was on the back of a good horse.

Brannon was surprised that Mrs. Mulroney had covered so much ground in such a little amount of time. He reached the top of the mountain and spotted her scooting among the scattered boulders and lightning-scarred trees.

"Mrs. Mulroney, wait! Mrs. Mulroney, we must go back to Broken Arrow Crossing!"

Sage picked his way through the rocks, and soon he was walking the horse beside her.

"Ma'am . . . we need to go back now."

"I simply can't stop. I must reach Dublin before supper." She picked up her pace.

"Ma'am, the shooting is all over. I'll give you a ride back to the cabin."

"Cabin?"

"The cabin, the barn, the children . . . remember?"

"Oh, children. Yes, we shall have children. After the wedding." She was almost running.

Brannon hesitated to touch the bewildered woman, but he finally swung off the horse and grabbed her by the shoulders. Looking her in the eyes, he shook her and said, "Peter is shot. He is seriously hurt. You've got to snap out of this. He needs your help! You've got to go help Peter. He almost died trying to save you!"

She stood for a moment staring back at Brannon. He could see her eyes, her face, her body relax.

"Mr. Brannon, we must hurry. Peter needs me."

Then she turned towards the horse and fainted.

Brannon rode up to the cabin carrying Mrs. Mulroney in his arms. Elizabeth met him on the porch.

"Is she alive?"

"She just fainted. Some cold water should bring her around. How's Mr. Mulroney?"

"Mr. Davis is dressing his wound. He has lost very much blood."

"How about Fletcher?"

Elizabeth smiled. "He doesn't want to talk about it."

"What?"

"He will heal quickly. Let me help with her."

They got Mrs. Mulroney into the cabin, and Elizabeth washed her face. In a moment the woman blinked her eyes open and looked around. Elizabeth finished cleaning her.

"I must help Peter!" she said, rising up quickly. She hurried towards the crawl hole to the barn and then turned back. "Elizabeth, thank you for helping me."

As she left, Brannon stared at Elizabeth.

He shook his head. "Is that the first time she ever thanked you?"

"And it is the first time she called me by my name."

"She's getting better."

"It has not been easy for her."

"I'm going to check on the injured. Then I'll get a shovel and go clean up the clearing."

"You will bury them?"

"Yeah, it's getting to be a habit."

Brannon entered the barn and found Everett Davis and Mrs. Mulroney kneeling down on the straw next to the injured man.

"Peter? How are you?"

"I'll survive. I have a good woman." The Irishman clasped his wife's hand.

Mrs. Mulroney sat at attention. "Mr. Davis, if you'll find another bandage, I need to tighten this wrap. And, Mr. Brannon, could you ask Elizabeth to bring Peter something to eat? A little broth will be nice. Mr. Fletcher," she called, "could you swing the door open a bit more? It's stuffy in here. Now, children, everything is all right. You may go outside and play."

Everett Davis and Brannon scooted over to Fletcher by the barn door.

"What do you think?" Brannon asked.

"Like the little lady said, everything's all right. Mulroney lost a lot of blood, but the bullet passed through his shoulder. As long as he can get some rest, he'll pull out of it. What did you say to the missus?"

"I just told her that her husband needed her. I don't know. I guess she just made up her mind to see it through. Sometimes a person has to just make up their mind." He turned to Fletcher. "Edwin, how about your wound? Where were you hit?"

"I guess the bullet came off the rocks," the Englishman reported. "Davis says it wasn't buried very deep. I'll tough it out."

Brannon looked at Everett Davis, then at Fletcher, and then back to Davis. "Everett, I never did hear him say just where he got shot."

The older man grabbed Brannon's arm and howled, "Well, it won't affect his dancin', but he'll have to ride standin' in the stirrups!"

"You two can jolly it up," Fletcher lectured, "but it's quite painful, actually. And a bit awkward. I mean, how do I write home about the nobility being wounded in a western shootout?"

Brannon grinned and pushed his hat to the back of his head. "Well, tell them you got caught in the relentless crossfire from ruthless desperadoes and took lead in the blind side before sending the villainous embodiment of evil to their just rewards."

"I say, that is good. Would you write that down?" Edwin asked.

"Col. Judson beat me to it."

"Col. Judson?"

"Ned Buntline. You know, the guy with the dime novels."

"Oh, well," Fletcher paused, "actually, I rather enjoyed that line. Perhaps later you might go over it again."

Brannon grabbed the shovel that leaned against some leather harnesses.

"Everett, look after the wounded. Me and Sage need to clean up the clearing."

"Brannon, did you ever think about being an undertaker?"

"Never. Where's Spotted Horse? Didn't he come in with Elizabeth?"

"Yeah, he went hunting for some meat. Elizabeth said it was necessary when you join a new camp to bring a present."

"Well, tell her I'll be in by dark."

Brannon mounted Sage and rode back out to where the Rutherford gang sprawled in the snow. Over near the trees where the snow had melted and the ground was fairly thawed, he dug one wide grave.

With Sage's help, he moved the bodies into the grave. Before he covered them up, Brannon paused and leaned on the shovel.

Lord, I didn't bring Everett's Bible because I didn't think these fellas were worthy of its words. I honestly don't know one good thing about them. I know they didn't hesitate to shoot innocent folks and hurt women, and, Lord, I just don't have much use for such as these. But it's not mine to say what they did or didn't do, so give them what they deserve.

With the speech finished, Brannon turned to the task of covering up the grave. He moved quickly, tossing shovel after shovel of red clay, mud, and sticks. He tamped the dirt down the best he could, smoothed down the surface, and tossed a few handfuls of pine needles on top, making it look like the rest of the area. Finally, he used his boot to scrape the mud off the shovel and remounted Sage.

From the saddle he peered back down at the grave.

Lord, it's me again. I've been thinking about what I said, and to tell You the truth, maybe these fellas ought to get a little better than they deserve. I mean, none of us deserve very much. We sure didn't deserve the baby in Bethlehem, and we didn't deserve what happened on the cross, nor did we deserve that empty grave on Easter day. So, Lord, have mercy on them. Have mercy on us all.

Spotted Horse had returned with a small deer to roast for the evening meal. He had built a large fire in front of the cabin and set up his camp on the front porch.

Brannon nodded at him as he rode over to the barn. He finished settling Sage in his stall, checked on the Mulroneys and then crawled through the wall into the cabin.

Everett Davis sat at the tablet pencil and paper in hands while Edwin Fletcher stood looking over his shoulder.

"Elizabeth? We've got plenty of room for your brother in the barn. No reason for him to stay out there." Brannon swung his leg over the bench and sat down beside Davis.

"That's what I told her," the older man offered.

"My brother will not come inside a wooden building. He does not like it indoors. He says he gets sick. Besides I'm afraid Mrs. Mulroney would get sick again if she looked up and saw my brother."

"Well, you might be right about that. How long will he be staying with us?"

"Until right after breakfast."

"Breakfast? You mean tomorrow?"

"Yes, tomorrow we will leave."

"Yeah, well, you know . . . I'm very happy you get to go home."

"Yes, so am I. Will you be going home, Mr. Brannon? Home to your ranch in Arizona?"

"I've got a feeling we might try hunting a little gold first," Brannon replied.

Everett Davis interrupted, "Now that's what me and

Fletcher was talking about. We drew up this mining claim. It says that the mine will be joint owned by the three of us and the kid. We work the mine, and he discovered it, so we split the fortune four ways. How does that sound?"

"Well, it sounds good providing we can find that cave again."

"Yes, well," Fletcher added, "I thought you could draw a map on how to get there."

He handed Brannon the pencil and paper.

"Well," he started in, "here's Tres Casas, and here's Brighton Pass. Now almost straight up here just beyond North Pass is the high end of the Little Yellowjacket. Somewhere along that is a box canyon and Charley Imhoff's claim . . . right, Everett?"

"Yep."

"Now over here to the east of the cabin are hot springs, about two ridges over and upstream. If we follow one of those creeks up a few miles, it turns almost a ninety-degree angle. It's probably going to be under water, but maybe we can divert the stream. Then, well, then we'll see what Providence has in store for us."

"What about Charley's notion about a box canyon up on the Little Yellowjacket?" Davis asked.

"Well, you can do what you want. But I'll take a chance on those nuggets that little Stephen brought in rather than a canyon that nobody's ever seen. The Rutherfords spent most of the winter up there and couldn't find it."

"Fletcher, what's your stake in this?" Everett Davis turned to the Englishman.

"I beg your pardon?"

"Well, it seems like you are pretty well-heeled. I'm not sure why you want to dig in the mud of Colorado."

"Because it's a whale of a lot more exciting than playing cricket," he scoffed.

Elizabeth scurried around the cabin gathering up what

few belongings she had made and been given during the winter. She bundled them and put them by the door. Then she spent most of the evening sitting out around Spotted Horse's fire.

Just before daylight it poured rain and didn't stop all day. Spotted Horse and Elizabeth decided to wait until the storm subsided.

On the fourth day after the rain began, they woke up to clear skies. The rain had melted most of the snow around the cabin, barn, and clearing. There were plenty of patches in the forest, along the arroyos, and up in the high mountains.

A few minutes after daylight, a bullet slammed against the side of the cabin, followed by the deep explosion of Spotted Horse's buffalo gun.

Stuart Brannon shoved open the door to the cabin and charged into the morning air with neither his hat nor his boots.

Spotted Horse was crouched down on the porch pointing the gun at the trail up from Brighton Pass.

Brannon thought he could see a wagon and team parked among the trees.

"Who's out there?" he yelled, holding his rifle out in front of him.

"The name's Wishy Boswick, and that's my cabin. You and your Indian friend are going to have to leave!"

Brannon turned to the cabin. "Everett! Get out here and tell Boswick to quit shooting!"

Davis called to Boswick, and soon the freight owner came walking across the clearing.

"It's been a rough winter, Wishy, and I had a little company."

Boswick looked up and down the gang at Broken Arrow Crossing. "So I see. I've been worried about you, Everett. We were told that Harlan Rutherford and a few like him we're going up to the Little Yellowjacket to bully their way into the claims. I would have expected them to stop here and give you trouble."

"Oh, they did."

"And you took care of them by yourself?"

"Not me," Davis replied. "That's Brannon's job."

"You a hired gun?" Wishy Boswick asked.

Everett Davis broke back in, "He's a gunman all right, but I don't think he's for hire."

"I'm going to need some good men to ride shotgun out of the goldfield," Wishy stated. "Are you looking for gold like every other man in the country or looking for a steady job?"

"I appreciate the offer, Boswick, but I'm not looking for a job," Brannon responded. "Is Brighton Pass open? We've got some folks who are mighty anxious to get back out of the mountains."

"Well, yes and no. See, I hired a dozen men to dig the snow out and open the pass to the goldfield up on the Little Yellowjacket. About four days ago at dark, we had her fairly clear so I brought the first wagonload of supplies for Broken Arrow Crossing through. Before daylight the next day it must have rained nine inches.

"The snow melted, and the ground thawed and turned to mud. Seems like one-third of Brighton Peak slid down on the roadway. It will be another week before I can get it opened up, provided Meyers can find another work crew."

"Lonnie Meyers still working for you?" Davis asked.

"Yeah, but he's about the only one. The twelve diggers who first opened up the pass tossed down their shovels and hightailed it straight up the mountain to look for gold. Anyway, I've got one load of supplies back there stuck in the mud. It should keep the cabin going for a while. Everett, I'll need you to stay and run the station until I get someone up here. There are over four hundred men hanging around Tres Casas waiting to waste their youth and their health in that Colorado mudhole."

"Sorry, Wishy, I cain't do it. I've got my own plans," Davis explained. "You know me, always trying to find another strike."

Boswick turned to Brannon and Fletcher, "Say, how would you two men like a job for the next couple weeks until I get—"

"Boswick," Brannon shrugged, "we'll be leaving this place ourselves. Sorry."

Suddenly, Peter Mulroney, leaning on his wife's shoulder, appeared at the door.

"Is the pass open?"

Brannon turned and spoke, "In just a few more days."

Mulroney continued, "They'll be a lot of folks coming through her, right?"

"Correct."

"The Mulroneys will be wanting to leave—" Brannon started to interrupt.

"We'd like to have the job. It's my wife and the kids and me. I ran a livery back in Ireland. I think I can do it."

"Mulroney!" Brannon cautioned, "What about the missus's health?"

"It was her idea. She refuses to travel another step."

"I'll give you two extra horses to use, all the supplies you need, and twenty-five dollars a month," Boswick offered.

"You got yourself a man," Mulroney nodded. "I'm a little peaked right now, but I'll be strong by next week."

"Everett, can you give me a hand with that stuck wagon? I pulled her over in a mudhole by accident when I saw this Indian in front of your cabin. I just knew you'd been bushwhacked."

"I'll give you a hand," Fletcher called and hurried to join up with the others.

Spotted Horse brought his horses around to the cabin as he and Elizabeth got ready to leave. Mrs. Mulroney rubbed her hands together and cleared her throat. "Elizabeth, I'm

. . . I'm sorry I was not more help around here. It's been a very rough winter for me."

The three Mulroney children stood behind their mother. Brannon held the reins of the horse. "Elizabeth, you have been a good friend and a brave partner. I'm glad you came to this cabin."

"Mr. Brannon, you have reminded me that life is often hard for many people, not only Indians. I like a man who will insist on doing right even in difficult times."

Brannon helped Elizabeth climb up on the horse. She laughed at Spotted Horse's words.

"My brother says you have spoiled me, and it will take a year to learn to become an Indian again."

"Well," Brannon searched for words to express his feelings, "you take care of that brave little warrior. Teach him to be as wise and as stubborn as his mother."

Elizabeth reached behind her and took the cradleboard off her back. "You have not said good-bye to the brave warrior." She handed Littlefoot down to Brannon.

It was the first time since the night of his birth that the baby had been touched by a white person. Brannon cradled Littlefoot in his left arm and let him hold on to his fingers. "Young man, you grow up strong and brave. Then you come find me, and I'll give you a job on the prettiest ranch you have ever seen."

Brannon gave the little one a gentle hug and returned him to Elizabeth.

"Mr. Brannon, in the camp of Chief Joseph they will hear of your strength and your honor."

"Elizabeth, in the deserts of Arizona they will hear of your courage and beauty."

She and Spotted Horse turned away from the cabin and walked the horses north.

Brannon stood and watched until he could no longer see

the smiling face of Littlefoot as he bounced on his mother's back.

Elizabeth did not turn around.

It took the combined efforts of Boswick, Fletcher, Davis, Brannon, the horse team, and Sage to pull the supply wagon out of the mud and get it to the barn. Mrs. Mulroney quickly dug into the supplies and began fixing a big dinner.

After everyone was stuffed with food, Fletcher and Everett Davis helped Boswick inventory his supplies. Brannon pulled Peter Mulroney aside.

"Peter, listen, if you folks are staying up here, you know you are welcome to head up there and help us dig for gold."

The Irishman grinned. "Thanks, but I was serious. My wife says she will not go one step further. We will stay here. Besides," he laughed, "Stephen is a partner, right? Well, one Mulroney is enough for any enterprise."

Brannon stood. "You are right, Stephen is a partner. I will need those gold samples to establish the claim."

"They're in the barn. They're yours."

Stuart Brannon walked out around to the barn. Everett Davis sorted through the supplies. Brannon and Fletcher examined Boswick's team of horses. Davis nodded at Brannon, and Brannon approached Wishy Boswick as he came down out of the hayloft.

"Boswick, are you open for business?"

"You need to buy some supplies?"

"Yeah, we were thinking it's about time to head up the hill ourselves," Brannon nodded.

"Gold fever, huh? Sure, men, what do you need?"

"Well, Everett's put together a list of food, pans, shovels, and picks, plus we will want those two horses and the two old saddles over on the wall."

"What? Take my horses?"

"You'll have more coming in a week, right?"

"Yes, but it will cost you. I can't just give them away."

Brannon strolled over to the stall next to Sage and picked up the jar of gold nuggets.

"How's this for collateral?"

Boswick took out a nugget and rolled it around in his hand. "Where on earth did you find this? Did you make it up to the Little Yellowjacket?"

"Wishy, you know better than to ask a man to reveal his claim," Everett Davis laughed. "Do we get the supplies or not?"

"Is this going to be a big strike?" Boswick grilled. "I mean, if it's going to be big, I'll need a lot more supplies up here and probably some—"

"Wishy," Everett laughed, "you'll be the first to know. Do we get the supplies?"

"Well, yes," Boswick droned as Davis poured out more nuggets in his hand.

It was barely daylight the next morning when Edwin Fletcher, Everett Davis, and Stuart Brannon saddled their horses and loaded up their gear.

Wishy Boswick and Mr. Mulroney met them at the corral outside the barn.

"You riding out early?" Boswick asked.

"Well, two of us are riding. Fletcher has decided to walk his horse for a while. At least until he learns to ride standing on his head," Davis roared.

Brannon pulled up on Sage and turned to Mulroney. "Tell that boy of yours we'll be back in a month or so with a report on how things are going at the Little Stephen Mine."

"He will like that. Mr. Brannon," Mulroney continued, "you saved me, my wife, and my children this winter. There are no rewards enough on earth to repay you."

"Then I'll have to wait for the ones in heaven," Brannon

laughed. "It has been a long winter. I'm beginning to sound like Davis."

With Fletcher walking his horse, the other two rode past the cabin and toward Broken Arrow Creek. They paused at the water's edge as Stuart Brannon rummaged through his saddle bags.

"Mr. Brannon! Mr. Brannon, wait!"

Mrs. Mulroney came running out of the front door of the cabin carrying something in her apron.

"Take these extra biscuits with you," she offered.

"Thank you, ma'am." Brannon took the bundle, tipped his hat, and shoved them into his gear bags. He pulled out a small, brass-framed picture.

Without looking at it, he began to coax Sage into the swirling stream.

"Mr. Brannon! Mr. Brannon!"

He turned in the saddle and rested his right hand on the cantle.

Mrs. Mulroney had come down by the water.

"Mr. Brannon, I believe winter is over, don't you?"

Stuart Brannon looked away from Mrs. Mulroney and stared at the smiling face in the brass-framed picture. After a deep sigh, he turned back to the woman. "Yes, ma'am, winter's over."

"Thank you for helping us make it through. May God have mercy on you, Mr. Brannon."

"I'm sure He will." Brannon spurred Sage across the rocky creek bed. "And may God have mercy on you, Mrs. Mulroney."